CW00863601

ECLAIRS FOR TEA

AND OTHER STORIES

by

Julia Blake

www.juliablakeauthor.co.uk

Table of Contents

Dedication

To so many people

My Parents, as always

Becky, for technical support and so much more

My Instagram family for encouragement and virtual hugs

And Francesca, my daughter, thank you for your patience

A Note for the Reader

This is a real mixed bag of goodies, and represents over a decade of scribbling. I had no idea what to do with this back catalogue of short stories, poetry and flash fiction, until a chance remark by a reader – that she couldn't read Lifesong, my novella, because it's only available as a download – made me wonder how true this was for other people. I determined to somehow get Lifesong out there as a paperback, but, wanted it to be part of a bigger collection, and the idea dawned to include it with all the other little bits and pieces I'd written over the years, a sort of smorgasbord of words.

Although novels will always be my first love, I do enjoy the reduced commitment of short stories, flash fiction and poetry. My poems are far from what could be termed high literature, there not being a cloud or a daffodil in sight, and I like to think my poetry is more every day, normal stuff, but, maybe they will appeal to all those every day, normal people out there, who perhaps like their poems to be less about abstract ideas, and more about things that touch us all – work, children, our family and friends.

Anyway, I hope you enjoy them, and, as ever, appreciate comments, thoughts or maybe even simple shout outs on my Facebook page, Julia Blake - Author.

You can also follow me on Instagram, and read my blogs and various book reviews on Goodreads.

Check out trailers for my books on my YouTube Channel - Julia Blake Author.

All the best ~ Julia Blake

Other Books
by the Same Author

The Book of Eve – a tale of secrets, betrayal and love

Lifesong – our world seen through the eyes of an alien

Becoming Lili – an ugly duckling, coming of age story, set in 90's Britain

ECLAIRS FOR TEA

AND OTHER STORIES

by

Julia Blake

Bedtime

Scabby knees, softened by pale, pink, bubbles.
She picks, morbid fascination in every line of her body.
Don't do that, I say, and hear an echo of my mother,
So many years ago, when I too, bore my scabs with pride.
She splashes me, chortling aloud with joy,
And I envy the wonderful spontaneity of a child's laugh,
Free of constraint, the shackles of respectability.

I lift her from the bath, and, swathed in oversized towel,
She shuffles, penguin like, from the room. Too heavy,
To carry now, I miss the feel of that small, sturdy, weight,
Nestled damply against my chest, arms around my neck.
Marvel at the perfection of her body, shiny with newness.
A computer on factory settings, untainted, uncorrupted,
By the toxins of the world, gorged on its own excesses.

Drying by the fire, flames leap in her eyes, and,
We talk, her and I, in this precious time before bed.
Mummy, how is a rainbow made, she asks, and I ponder.
A serious question, deserves a serious reply, and I fumble,
At half-remembered science, light refraction and rain,
Until she stops me, eyes wide with the wisdom of youth,
I expect unicorns make them. I agree, it is a good answer.

Warmly dressed in pyjamas, I tuck her into her pink bed.
Eyes already heavy, skin golden,
In the comforting bloom of the nightlight.
And I wish, she could stay for longer.
In this magical world, where Santa will always visit,
Where the existence of Unicorns is without doubt,
And a Teddy can really talk.
The little brown bear is tucked firmly under her chin.
He looks at me, and, his eyes, dim with cataracts
From one to many trips through the wash,
Twinkle, as if to say, don't worry, I'll take it from here

TAPROOT

As war raged in the skies above, Meg fought her own battle against growing up and her fears for her brother

Taproot

25th August 1940

This has been the worst week of my life...and the strangest

Sun warm on the red, brick, wall. It had been a very hot summer, things had grown, ripened. Just as well, without the fruit and vegetables Craddock managed to grow, mumbling and complaining about his back, his age, the state of the world in general, food would have been scarce.

Meg lay, silent and motionless, in her favourite spot in the whole garden, where the runner beans grew, lank and twisting, over eight foot canes tied into living wigwams. It was her place. A place to hide when things became too much. When emotions and physical sensations threatened to overwhelm, choking her with their intensity. Meg had spent many hours there this summer.

It had been a summer of change, charged with feelings, new and unbearable as, snake like, she felt her old self sloughing off, being left behind in a world of hair ribbons and toys, childish concerns and joys. She was growing. Into what, Meg wasn't sure.

There had been those terrible, amazing, few days in June, when all looked lost. The bulk of the British Army, tattered and beaten, huddled on a shore so achingly close, and yet, a million miles away. The overwhelming patriotic rush, when nearly all were saved, hearing Charlie had been among them. Those precious few days, when he came home on leave.

"Don't ask me," was all he'd said, in reply to her fevered questions. "Don't."

Meg looked into his eyes, fled from the hell she saw there, hastily veered away to safer subjects, the house, the garden, the rapidly declining health of their grandmother. Anything, other than the war raging across the water. The war he would soon have to go back to.

They talked of the future, of Meg's inability to leave their home, her terror of anything that lay beyond the safety of the garden's high, stone, walls.

"You'll never have to leave here, not if you don't want to," he vowed, his blue eyes intense. His reassurances were balm to her pressured soul. Helped her forget, for a while, the way others looked at her, forget knowing they were whispering about her, judging, condemning her as odd, different.

"But, you'll inherit when grandmother...goes. You'll marry, what if your wife doesn't want your stupid baby sister cluttering up the place?"

"Then I won't marry her," he laughed. "How could I love someone, who doesn't love you as well? No, you'll be auntie to my children, great auntie to theirs. This is your home, Meg, I know what it means to you. You're a part of this place. It's like you have a taproot going down into its soil. If anyone tried to uproot you, you'd die."

"But..." she began, thoughts flying to the war, a war he would soon have to return to.

"I'll always look after you, Meg," her brother promised, and she knew he meant it. But, what if he couldn't keep that promise, what it...?

Then he'd gone. She was left alone again. All too quickly, the old fears crept back. The insecurity and worry for herself, her future. When her grandmother died, as it was increasingly obvious she would, she'd be alone. There was Craddock in the garden, and Mrs Craddock in the house, but they didn't count. They weren't family. They weren't Charlie.

Fingers dug into sun-baked soil, dusty, warm, clogging under her nails, panic eating at her abdomen. Those strange, cramping, pains, Meg couldn't understand, but was afraid of.

Hair spread on the dirt, Meg opened her eyes, stared into the sun for as long as she dared, then looked around the garden, through vision made gloriously rosy. Blinking back tears, saw movement in the cabbage patch. Sitting up, so fast it made her head spin, she stared, rubbing grimy hands over disbelieving eyes.

There was a woman, an old woman, tending a rose bush, right in the middle of Craddock's cabbages.

Blurry, indistinct, the figure seemed oblivious to Meg, as she proficiently deadheaded the gorgeous, plump, pink, blooms. Could Meg smell their scent? It almost seemed she could. Slowly, she rose to her feet, moved silently towards the apparition. It was an old woman, very old, her face drooping into lines of experience, her hair, loose and silvered, under the wide brimmed, tatty, straw, hat. The rest of her clothes were odd, but looked comfortable, perfect for gardening on a hot, airless, day. Wide legged, cotton, trousers, a matching, sleeveless, top and stout gloves.

"Hello?" whispered Meg, uncertain if she wanted to woman to respond or not. Shakily, she reached out a hand, so close now, she could touch the woman's arm. There was nothing there, her touch passed through air. Stumbling back, she cried out in disbelief, and the woman vanished.

"You alright, Miss?" It was Craddock, wheeling a barrow around the corner of the wall, coming upon her standing there, right in the middle of his cabbages, hand outstretched, a stricken expression on her face.

"What?" too stunned to be polite, Meg turned startled eyes upon him.

"You look like you've seen a ghost, Miss."

A ghost? Fear clutched at her guts. Mouth twisting with pain, her hand automatically rubbed at her swollen middle. Craddock's eyes followed her movement, and Meg saw the look on his face change from mild concern, to acute awkwardness.

"Reckon you'd better go indoors and see the Missus, she'll sort you out," he mumbled, averting his gaze, his face a course, brick, red. Not understanding, Meg looked down, saw the blood on her skirt.

Mrs Craddock 'sorted her out', during a painful half hour, which embarrassed them both hugely, and left her baffled with mortified confusion. She was, apparently, a woman now. Fully equipped with the necessary, shameful, paraphernalia, Meg was given an aspirin, and put to bed with a hot water bottle. Alone, she thought about what she'd seen, and wondered...

All the next day, and the next, the planes battled overhead, screaming their rage at each other.

"Is it thunder?" her grandmother mumbled, confused, lost in a disordered landscape of her own mind's making.

"Yes, Gran," Meg agreed, quietly. "It's thunder."

She escaped to the garden, buried her head in her hands, tried to drown out the awful sounds. Knowing, men from both sides were dying up there, wondering where Charlie was, if he was safe. She wondered what would happen to her, and the house, if anything happened to him, despising herself for such shallow, selfish, thoughts.

And all that week, Meg constantly saw...her...came to long for glimpses of her calm, placid, face, the pleasure the woman obviously gained from tending her beautiful garden. A garden, which was plainly Meg's garden, but, was different, somehow... Bursting with fragrant, stunning, flowers, there wasn't a single vegetable in sight. And Meg wondered, how that could be.

The woman never saw her, never heard her. After a while, Meg stopped trying to get her attention, was content to merely be in her presence. Soothed by the smallness of her movements, her attention intensely focused upon her plants.

Every day, that terrible week, she saw her, and, every day, the hell raged overhead. Once, an enemy plane came down, less than a mile from the house. Mrs Craddock was full of the story, it's pilot had, apparently, died on impact, but still...

"We could all have been murdered in our beds," Mrs Craddock declared, voice thrilling at the thought of it.

Meg thought about it in bed that night. Imagined, the pilot's last moments alive. What must have gone through his head, as he saw the earth racing up to meet him? Again, she thought of Charlie, so far away, longed for the security of his presence – I'll always look after you, Meg.

On Wednesday, Mrs Craddock sent her out to pick runner beans for dinner. Carefully, slowly, she worked her way down the rows. The beans had to be exactly the right size. Too small, and Mrs Craddock would moan they weren't worth bothering about. Too large, and they'd be stringy.

The sun was hot on her head, she'd forgotten her hat. Meg thought about the hat the old woman wore, wondered where she could get a hat like that. Then, she heard the bicycle bell, turned, saw the telegram boy.

The world stopped.

Pressure pushed at her eardrums. She dropped the basket, spilling the beans on the ground, where Craddock would later pick them up, shaking his head in understanding pity.

Panic stabbed everywhere. Her heart. Her stomach. Her head.

Meg heard someone softly moaning, realised it was herself, as the boy rode past, heading for the house. Forcing her legs to move, she stumbled down the path, saw Mrs Craddock at the door, apprehension creasing her face.

"Give me," Meg gasped, snatched the small, hateful, envelope from the boy's startled grasp. Speedily, he remounted his bicycle and rode away. Unhappy experience, had taught him not to hang around.

Captain Charles Bellingham, missing in action, presumed dead

No matter how many times, Meg read and re-read the words, they were always the same. She didn't understand, these were not the words she wanted to read. So why, were they so stubbornly intent on staying the same.

Charlie was dead. He couldn't be. She refused to believe it – I'll always look after you, Meg – she clung to his promise, like a drowning man clings to a lifeline.

People came. The doctor. The vicar. Mrs Bingham, the local Red Cross leader, and all-round busybody. Her tongue, hinged in the middle, flapped, with well-meaning, inadequate, platitudes. To them all, Meg presented the same blank, dry eyed, stare.

She'd lost Charlie. What was going to happen to her now?

She couldn't eat, could barely force the tea Mrs Craddock made her, past the lump in her throat. For three days, she lay as one in a coma, unresponsive, unfeeling – I'll always look after you, Meg. He'd lied.

Finally, she had to get out, felt the walls of her room closing in on her. Could no longer bear to breathe air steeped in her own misery. Meg chose a time, when Mrs Craddock was busy elsewhere, slipped down the stairs, out the side door, and into the garden.

Would the old woman be there? Meg needed to see her, to feel her calmness, her serenity. Back steady against warm, red, bricks, Meg slid down the wall to sit and wait, all day, if necessary. Her fingers poked at the bloat of her stomach, hating the messiness of being a woman, the awful responsibility of it.

She appeared, as usual, yet, not as ethereal as before. She seemed sharper, more vivid, her outline distinct. Meg could even see her feet, clad in practical, canvas, shoes, battered and solid, they rooted her firmly to the earth of the garden, like a taproot.

Meg exhaled again, letting go the painful breath she'd been holding inside for days, bruising her lungs, clogging her throat.

Suddenly, the woman stopped, exclaiming impatiently, as she examined a badly scratched arm. Sucking the wound, she slowly raised her head and turned to look at Meg. No, not at her exactly, more like through her, those faded blue eyes searching the wall.

"I know you're there, Meg," she said. "And I know what you're going though. But, you must listen to me, and you must believe. It's going to be alright. Charlie isn't dead, it's a mistake. He's hurt, oh, so badly hurt, the war is over for him. He's coming home soon, and you must take care of him. You must be the one to look after him, Meg, but, I promise you, everything is going to be alright. Now go, hurry, back to the house, they're looking for you with the news. Run, Meg, run."

She ran. Hope exploding in her heart like a bomb. Halfway there, saw Mrs Craddock rushing towards her, waving a small envelope like a flag.

"Miss," she cried. "Oh, Miss!"

25th August 2010

What a very strange week this has been. The children went back to their busy lives around the world last week. For the first time, in what seems months, I'm alone again. Not that I mind, of course not, I've never minded being alone, and appreciate how lucky I am, to have a family who wish to spend so much time with great aunt

Margaret. Still, it seems a long time to wait, until the end of October, when they'll be back, for the traditional Halloween and Bonfire Night weekend.

I've been busy in the garden all week, there was so much to do. I've neglected the roses terribly, and have had to spend many hours deadheading and tidying them. It's odd, beyond Mrs Smith, who came in on her usual days, and Fitch, who came to cut the grass on Wednesday, I haven't seen a soul all week, yet, I haven't felt alone. On the contrary, all week I've felt as if I was being watched in the garden. Not in a sinister way, no, more in a benign, friendly sort of fashion.

There was a programme about the Battle of Britain on BBC2 last night, which brought it all back. Is it really seventy years? It seems hard to believe, but, I suppose it must be. I remember that summer so vividly, the summer I was thirteen. I'm eighty-three now, and, sometimes, it seems the memories of those days are clearer than those of last week, the fear, the pressure, the uncertainty about the future, especially my own...

It was warm for late August, global warming seeming to have had the opposite effect on British summers of late, she reflected wryly. Remembering, with a pang, the endless, scorching, summers of her childhood.

She was deadheading again, thinking fondly how roses were worth all the work and worry, for those few, brief, weeks in summer, when they rewarded you with glorious blooms like these. Her mind wandered to the programme she'd watched last night, how distant the jerky, black and white, footage made it all seem.

Her distraction made her careless, and a thorn scratched painfully, raising a bleeding welt down her forearm. Exclaiming with pain, she sucked away the hurt, and a memory struck with the force of a hurricane. Raising her head, she scanned the nearby wall, not seeing anything, but knowing, all the same, that she was there, seventy years ago, watching herself prune these very roses.

"Meg," she began, gently. "I know you're there..."

The End...

My Friend's Father

My friend's father,
Was considerably older than my own,
A tall, slightly stooped, figure,
With blue eyes that gazed beyond me.
As if seeing things, I could never, ever, know.

My friend's father,
Had an accent,
Exotic in its unfamiliarity.
It hinted at a time far away,
And a place long ago,
Of happenings beyond my understanding.

My friend's father,
Was called papa by my friend,
And, sometimes, I secretly wished
For him to be my father too,
Coveting his foreignness for myself.

My friend's father,
Had a past, never to be spoken of,
Unlike my father, who'd cheerfully tell,
Of a boyhood spent working the farm,
That Teddy boy youth who'd courted my mother.

My friend's father,
Trembled tea into his saucer,
When once, innocently, I asked,
The numbers quivering on his wrist,
Blued with age. Faded, but never forgotten.

Don't Tread on the Cracks

Don't tread on the cracks, Mary Jane,
Because if you fall, we'll have to make a claim.
And hanging baskets must go, because it's been said,
One might fall on someone's head.

At school, Mary Jane, attend teacher well,
And if she upsets you, run home and tell.
Then, perhaps, we can sue the school,
For breaking some necessary PC rule.

Conker's have been banned, just think of the danger.
And at Christmas, you won't be singing away in a manger.
It's simply not fair to the ethnic minority,
And not causing offence must be our top priority.

On sports day, Mary Jane, don't bother to try.
For if we have no losers, then no child will cry.
Don't run, don't play, for you may trip.
Don't climb a tree, in case your clothes you rip.

Pedophiles and pervs lurk behind every tree.
So, your childhood must be spent in captivity.
You must stay alert, Mary Jane, stay very afraid,
And don't eat wild berries, they might have been sprayed.

Your life will be crammed with things to be done,
So many extra-curricular activities, there's no time for fun.
And as for your breakdown, from pressure and stress,
Don't worry, Mary Jane, we'll get the best child therapist.

And when you're grown, and look at the world we've made.
Where no one is happy, and everyone's afraid.
Where no one ever fails, so no one ever succeeds,
A world with no flowers, just millions of identical weeds.

You'll look around and wonder, my god, what've we done?
What happened to the laughter, what happened to the fun?
But don't bother trying to thank me, I did it all for you.
Only don't tread on the cracks, Mary Jane, you just might
  fall right through.

ECLAIRS

FOR TEA

**There was something very important
Kevin had told her not to forget.
If only she could remember what it was**

Eclairs for Tea

Overnight, it had snowed, great, billowy, drifts, that covered the lawn and trees.

At breakfast, Kevin, one of the staff, smiled at her excitement, and covertly dropped a toffee in her lap.

"Don't tell anyone," he whispered. "But cook's making eclairs for tea." He winked at her greedy gasp, before hurrying off to serve the others.

She liked Kevin.

Later, wrapped in layers of warm clothing, Nan took her out for her walk. A single row of footprints, aggressive in the otherwise untouched lawn, led into the woods. Leaving Nan stumbling behind on decrepit knees, she tracked them, hurrying until Nan's strident tones faded.

The footprints terminated at the old quarry, strictly forbidden to her, and made all the more attractive for the ban. Carefully, feet trembling with anticipated shock, she edged closer, to where she could see the edge had recently crumbled. Heart pounding in her chest, she peered over.

Far below, Kevin lay, twisted and broken, crimson soaking the white. His eyes, dark with pain in a bleached face, fixed on her, focused.

"Harriet," he gasped. "Go fetch help, there's a good girl. Run! Don't forget, fetch help!"

She ran, lungs exploding, until she collided with Nan, grabbed at her, breathlessly gabbling. "There's a man, in the woods..."

"Harriet," Nan's lips purse crossly. "What have you been told about lying? There's no man, there never is. Now, come on, it's freezing out here, it's time to go back."

That afternoon, Roddy came for tea. They played snap, whilst Nan bustled about, putting logs on the fire, drawing the thick curtains against the blustering snowstorm, the ever-increasing cold, which begged for entry.

As she laid the table for tea, Roddy looked around in surprise.

"No Kevin tonight, Mrs Nanders?"

"No," Nan frowned with remembered annoyance. "He went on his break after breakfast, and hasn't been seen since."

Kevin? He'd told her something to remember, something very important. What had it been? Oh yes...

"There's eclairs for tea."

"Really?" Roddy patted her hand, his flesh firm and young, hers ancient. "That's nice, Gran."

In her pocket, she clutched the toffee in her palm. She liked Kevin. She hoped he came back soon,

The End...

Nan

Flowery cotton pinny, crossed over shoulders
Broad enough to cope, with whatever life delivered.
Warm, baggy skin, from which arose, Nana smells.
Oil of Ulay and Pears soap. Yardley talc,
Dusted into crevices etched by toil and hardship,
A life of thoughtless, engrained to the bone, thrift.
So, second nature, so instinctive,
It made a mockery of our modern, credit crunch notions,
Of make do and mend.

Kitchen scraps in the pig pail,
Ready to feed those two shadowy monsters,
Which snuffled and grunted, over in the big shed,
Terrifying, yet, at the same time, attracting,
Inquisitive eyes, and brave little fingers
Poked through railings, only to run, shrieking,
When the monsters came to investigate.

Nothing was wasted,
Even crusts from a faddy child's plate,
Were soaked in milk, ready to make bread pudden'.
Nan's bread pudden, the stuff of legends,
A solid brick of pure fat and carbs.
Hearty enough to stick to ribs,
And anywhere else it touched,
Pockets of sweet, succulently plump, sultanas,
Exploding into melting, oozing warmth on your tongue,
Made every mouthful, a thrill of discovery.

Long days, exploring, and claiming as my own,
The hay meadows which surrounded Nan's house.
A child's paradise,
complete with hordes of village children.
Common as muck, my mother would sniff,
Yet I didn't care, gladly followed where they led,
The secrets they shared, of birds' nests and dens,
Of hidden streams, and the absolutely,
Bestest ever trees for climbing.

The sting of witch hazel,
On green grazed knees and elbows,
Tacit agreement reached, parents did not need to know,
I'd been breaking rules, and ascending the heights again.
Lunches eaten in the open,
Usually in the branches of a tree.
Sandwiches of white Mother's Pride, thick sliced,
Slathered with marg and jam.
No thought given to cholesterol and calories,
But, somehow, we thrived, and grew healthy on it.

Tumbling home, ravenous as puppies,
The setting sun picking out
Nan's windows with gold,
Thoughts gladly turning tea-wards.
Toast made on the fire, dripping with butter,
Hard boiled eggs and salad. Cheddar,
So mature it stung the eyes,
Home-made pickle and salad cream.
And, best of all, cake. At least four kinds, all home-made,
No shop bought cake ever disgraced Nan's table.

The unforgiving hardness of the pew beneath my bottom,
Sitting beside Nan in chapel on a Sunday.
Her thin, reedy, voice, piping out her favourite hymns,
Head bobbing under her Sunday best hat.
Nan's hats, of which she had a succession,
Each one more hideous than the one before.
And yet, there was a strange kind of comfort, in knowing,
That time may end, and civilisations crumble into dust,
But Nan's hats would endure.

That occasional, much longed for, treat,
Of sleeping at Nan's.
Heavy candlewick bedspread, old creaky wooden bed.
Coconut matting, cold underfoot,
The squat china po, and rose patterned oil lamp,
Casting kinetic, spine chilling, shadows on the ceiling.

Torchlight under the covers, heavy over my head,
Listening for the comforting boom of Big Ben striking ten,
Hearing the slow, ponderous, tread on the stairs,
Hurriedly feigning sleep,
Book thrust guiltily down by my toes.

The lamp being dimmed, until the world shrank,
And there was only that yellow circle of light,
And the soft, night time sounds of Nan,
Sleeping across the hall.

Morning Madness

Alarm jangles.
Groan, moan,
Ache, Wake!
Brace yourself,
Manic child,
Bed bouncing,
Springs creaking,
You shout,
Child pouts.

Breakfast ritual,
Toast, jam,
Milk spilled,
Tea gulped.
Bathroom chaos,
Toothpaste squirted,
Slimy soap,
Damp towels,
Hairbrush attack!

Lunches made,
Cats fed,
Dishwasher loaded,
Hurry, hurry!
Sergeant mummy,
Barking orders,
Move it!
Move it!
Go, go!

Keys found,
Bag packed,
Homework lost!
Where? Where?
Homework found!
Door slams.
Left behind,
Empty house,
Silently relaxes.

The Dinner Party

Charles prided himself on having the most interesting mix of guests at his dinner parties, But, has he gone too far this time?

The Dinner Party

Charles prided himself on hosting excellent dinner parties. The food was never less than exquisite, the wines subtle, and complementary to whatever culinary delights his chef had produced. The dining room and table were always the last word in sophisticated elegance, providing his guests with a visual feast, which paid homage to Charles's firm belief that 'the first bite is with the eye'.

As for the guests' themselves...ah...here, Charles really excelled himself. He chose with an almost fanatical care, and had often paraphrased the famous William Morris quote by stating 'have no one in your home, you do not believe to be beautiful, or know to be interesting'. His dinner parties, therefore, always comprised of an eclectic mix of witty, sophisticated, highly intelligent and interesting individuals. It was well known in society, Charles would have absolutely no compunction about only inviting one half of a couple, if he found the other half dull, ignorant, or simply not suitable for a particular mix of guests he had planned.

As Charles surveyed the large, circular, table laid with seven places, one last time before his guests arrived, he felt a quiet, smug, satisfaction as he mused over the place cards. A top politician, known for his forthright opinions, a visiting American comedian, whose dry, sarcastic, humour mostly aimed at his compatriots, had made him a bigger success in Britain than at home, a retired explorer whose quiet, self-depreciating, stories of discovery and adventure were always guaranteed to captivate and charm; an Italian opera singer, a magnificent, fiery, diva, with an earthy, almost peasant, outlook on life, which was exhilarating and refreshing, and that brought him to his last two guests.

Here, Charles paused, looking at the last two place cards. Had he been too naughty placing them side-by-side? He still had time to re-arrange, but no, his hand fell back to his side, and a wry smile crept onto his face. He had cast the dice, it would be interesting to see where it fell.

Charles looked around the mingled guests with private satisfaction. They were assembled in the drawing room, drinks in hand, awaiting the arrival of the last two guests, and already conversation was free-flowing and animated.

The Italian diva and the explorer were discussing Africa, both appearing to enjoy the other's different perspective on the same locations; the comedian and the politician were having a spirited debate on the Anglo/American relationship, in which both men seemed to be advocates for the other's country. Yes, it was a good start to the evening, just two more guests to come.

As if on cue, the doorbell rang. Charles quietly excused himself, slipped away to answer it. Laura was flustered at being late as usual, and Charles smiled indulgently, as she hurried in, still trying to cram too much into a small, beaded, evening bag, trailing a pashmina she clearly hadn't the faintest notion what to do with. His smile deepened, as he watched her stop by the hall table, dump her bag down, take out a pair of earrings and clip them on, running a hand through her short, tousled, hair she finally turned to him with a big smile.

'Hello, Charles darling. There we go, ready for action at last.'

'Laura, my sweet. Lovely to see you again. Tell me, do you have any eye make-up in that little bag of yours?'

With a frown, Laura peered in the mirror, then gave a squeal of horror, as she realised, in her haste, only one eye had been made up. The doorbell rang again. She pulled a face at him, gathered up her belongings, and fled into the cloakroom.

Shaking his head, Charles went to admit his final, tardy, guest. Darling Laura, they'd been friends since Oxford. She had been his rock, a staunch defender through those difficult times, when his family, his father especially, were finding it hard to come to terms with his sexuality.

Charles paused, hand on the door, was it fair? What he was about to do to Laura? Yes, hate him for it, she may, but Charles knew this was something Laura had to do. Opening the door to his last guest, Charles ushered him quickly into the drawing room.

'Let me introduce you to everyone, Simon, and then I'll get you a drink.' As he smoothly and urbanely made the introductions, Charles was acutely aware he was waiting for Laura's return. Last minute nerves at the enormity of what he'd done, causing his palms to go clammy, his heart to race a little within his overlarge frame. There was a sudden gasp from the door. Charles looked up to see Laura, frozen in place, blue eyes wide and fixed in shock.

'Simon Mills! What the hell are you doing here?'

Charles, watching him closely, saw a flicker of something in Simon's eyes, before his composure steadied.

'Laura, darling,' he drawled. 'Still as blunt as ever, I see. I was invited, by my very good friend, Charles.'

Those iced blue eyes now turned accusingly onto Charles, who shrugged, apologetically. 'I felt it was time you two buried the hatchet, and got over this nonsense. You both move in the same social circles, share the same friends, it would be nicer, for everyone, if you two could at least be civil to each other.'

Charles was horribly aware of the other guests' interest, the opera singer, in particular, listening with unabashed fascination. Laura drew herself up, looked at Charles with utter contempt.

'Nicer? Nicer for whom? Do you know, Charles, sometimes you can be a completely insensitive prick!'

Turning on her heel, she marched towards the door. Charles was horrified, never, in all his scheming, had he envisioned this scenario. He opened his mouth to speak, but Simon's sarcastic tone stopped him.

'That's right, Laura, run away as usual. You never were

any good at standing up for what you believed in, or fighting to keep what's important to you.'

Laura froze at the door, there was a collective gasp of horrified fascination from the other guests, then a deathly hush descended on the room. Charles's heart was in his mouth, as he looked at Laura's stiff, expressionless, back.

Slowly, she turned, her mouth tight, face drained of all colour, save for two red spots of anger, high on her cheekbones.

'And just what the hell is that supposed to mean?' Eyes glittering, she spat the words out.

Simon shrugged, 'I mean, why don't you for once try acting your age, instead of behaving like a wronged maiden in some Victorian melodrama. You've spent the last ten years avoiding me and hiding from me. Quite frankly, I'm sick of it all. Charles is right, it's time this thing was finished and settled between us, once and for all.'

'I have not been hiding from you! You presume too much importance for yourself, Simon. I haven't given you a second thought in ten years, or, if I have, it was only to think what a lucky escape I had.'

'Prove it.'

'What?'

'Prove you're not too scared to be in same room as me. Stay and have dinner. Show me you've grown up enough, to act in a mature and sensible manner.'

'Alright then, I will. Charles!'

Charles, whom, up until this point, had been listening to the exchange, rather the way spectators watch play at Wimbledon, snapped to attention.

'Laura?'

'Show me where I'm sitting, and let me get this ridiculous test out the way, so I can show this...this...' here, Laura's pretty mouth made a moue of disgust, 'Person, that I am under no circumstances, afraid of him!'

With that, she marched into the dining room, the other guests trailing uncertainly in her wake, leaving Charles and Simon to follow. Charles turned to Simon, in time to see a flash of triumphant admiration in his eyes.

'Dangerous game you're playing here, Charles, old boy,' he muttered. 'Not quite sure what you're hoping to achieve by it all, but, maybe you're right, it is time this was finished, once and for all...'

During the first course, Charles despaired of anything being resolved. Although sitting next to each other, Laura and Simon did not so much as even exchange glances, and the hostile silence between them was so thick, conversation between the other guests became stilted and awkward.

After the plates had been cleared away by the silently, efficient catering staff, and the fish course served, Charles decided to take matters into his own hands, and asked Laura how her latest book was coming along. If there was one thing guaranteed to make Laura talk, it was her extremely successful series of romantic novels.

'Very well, thank you for asking Charles. It's being released in June, and the publishers seem very happy with it.'

'And its title?'

'Love In Mind'. All of Laura's novels so far had the title Love In... Charles personally found them light and too clichéd for his taste, but, women everywhere lapped them up, and they earned Laura a comfortable income.

'Ahh!' exclaimed the opera singer, leaning across the table, her magnificent cleavage warm in the candlelight. 'You are Laura Hamilton? The Laura Hamilton? But, how magnificent, I have read every one of your books, they are superb. I find them intensely relaxing between shows, pure...how do you say it... escapism.'

Laura preened, self-confidence visibly flooding back into her.

'Thank you, it's very kind of you to say so.'

'Turgid rubbish,' Simon snorted.

Silence descended once more over the table, as Laura turned flinty cold eyes to him. 'I'm sorry, did you say something?'

'I said, turgid rubbish. I can't believe people waste good money buying such tripe, they'd be better off spending the money on lottery tickets – at least they're better entertainment value.'

'Delighted, though I am, Simon, that you managed to find someone to read one of my books to you, I do not appreciate such comments. My books sell very well, so obviously, most people do not agree with you.'

'By 'most people' I assume you're referring to the bored and lonely housewife brigade, who use your novels as a little, light relief, from scrubbing the kitchen floor.'

'Your comments are not only inaccurate and insulting to me, they are also extremely sexist and insulting to women, but then, why should I expect anything better from a man like you!'

'What do you mean, a man like me?' There was suddenly a dangerous edge to Simon's voice.

'I mean, a man like you who regards women as second-class citizens, who treats them like library books, to be borrowed for a short time, and then discarded when you've finished with them.'

'That's a bit low, even for you, Laura.'

'Yes, well, the truth hurts, doesn't it Simon?'

'Truth? Tell me Laura, what the hell would you know about the truth? You live in a fantasy world of make-believe heroines, where it always ends in marriage and happiness for all.'

'And what's wrong with that?'

'What's wrong with it? What's wrong with it, is it's all a lie, a big con; you sell desperate women a fantasy, a dream of happy ever after which doesn't exist. Marriage – the answer to all life's problems, hah, that's a joke.' He turned to the comedian. 'Who was it who said marriage was a great institution but who wants to live in an institute?'

'Ten years has made you even more cynical, Simon. I'm sorry you feel that way, but, for many people marriage works, and is the only viable way to live their lives.'

'I prefer to think of myself as a realist,' Simon retorted. 'The truth is, we've all been brainwashed into thinking if you don't get married and produce the requisite 2.4 children, there's something wrong with you. Well, I for one, am fed up with constantly having to apologise for being single, I'm single because I want to be. Who, in their right minds, would willingly place their happiness in someone else's hands?'

'When two people love each other, then marriage is the natural expression of that love, a commitment made to all, that they belong only to each other...'

'Only until something better comes along,' Simon interrupted. 'Have you looked at the statistics lately Laura? They kind of burst your cosy, romantic, bubble. Most married couples are all busy cheating away on each other, or making each other's lives a living hell, and as for the divorce figures...hah, what is it now, half of all marriages end in divorce? Them's not good odds, Laura.

'Maybe the pressures of modern life do put a strain on marriages. You say half of all marriages end in divorce, but, half don't, 50% of all marriages succeed, them's good odds, Simon.'

'It makes me sick, the sheer waste of money, I mean, what does the average wedding come in at now? £20,000 plus, just for one day? How many couples, actually bother, to think beyond the big I Do, to the lifelong sentence they've signed themselves up for? The number of weddings I've been to, and bought very expensive gifts for, I might add, where the marriage itself has lasted less than ten years. I should have asked for the gift back.'

'I agree that weddings themselves have got a little out of hand, but...'

'You see...'

'But, there is nothing more beautiful than two people swearing to love each other for all eternity, in a mutually binding ceremony, be it religious or civil, it doesn't have to be fancy or cost the earth. The most charming and sincere wedding I ever went to, was probably the one that cost the least.'

'Ok, I will agree sometimes people want to be with each other, but, instead of getting married and ruining the relationship, why don't they celebrate every year they successfully spend together.'

'Now you're being ridiculous. And anyway, what about children?'

'What about them?'

'Would that be a very stable background for them to be brought up in?'

'How many children do you know are brought up within stable marriages? No, their parents are all too busy having affairs, or fighting or divorcing to care much about what they're doing to the children. People have no idea what it's like to be a child within a situation like that, if they did, they'd think twice before getting married, and save everyone the trouble.'

Laura stared at him, sudden understanding and sympathy flooding her face; she reached out and placed a hand softly on his arm. 'Oh Simon, was that what it was like for you?'

Simon bristled, shrugging her hand off. 'All I'm saying, is it's ridiculous to gamble your happiness on someone else. Why risk it?'

'Why risk it?' replied Laura, softly, looking intently into his eyes. 'Why, for love Simon. When you love someone, you'd risk everything for them.'

Simon turned away from her gaze, pain twisting his mouth. 'Well, you didn't risk it for me, did you.'

'I would have done, Simon, if you'd let me, I'd have risked everything for you.'

The silence around the table was deafening, all eyes on Simon and Laura, who, in turn, appeared to only have eyes for each other.

'You never said...'

'I tried, Simon, but you seemed so distant, you shut me out, wouldn't talk...'

'I thought you didn't love me anymore.'

'Not love you anymore? Oh, Simon, you were my world. I couldn't bear it, I seemed to be losing you, especially when...I needed you so much that weekend, but you wouldn't talk to me.'

'That weekend? Oh god, Laura, my mother had tried to commit suicide again, another one of her cries for help, I needed some time to myself, to get my head together. You phoned me, practically demanded I ask you to marry you, right there and then. I'd come straight from the hospital, where I'd seen the evidence of what a messed-up marriage can do to you, and I just couldn't cope with it. All I said, was could you give me some space, next thing I knew, you were gone, you wouldn't talk to me, you returned my letters unopened, our friends seemed to have turned against me, and wouldn't tell me anything. In the end, I gave up.'

'But...I thought you wanted me out of your life, I thought you'd guessed what I wanted to talk to you about, although I knew what your answer was going to be, you'd made it quite plain what your feelings were on that score.'

'What? What score?' Simon's confusion was evident. 'What are you talking about, Laura?'

'When I asked you to marry me, Simon, I'd just found out I was pregnant.'

'Pregnant? Good god, Laura! Why on earth didn't you simply tell me? Why all the silly games?'

'Why do you think, Simon? Don't you remember the conversation we had about women who accidentally got pregnant? You said, there was no such thing as an accidental pregnancy, that it was usually the woman trying to trap the man into marriage, and that, it was a good thing, abortions were so easy nowadays. How do you think I felt when I found out I was accidentally pregnant? I didn't dare tell you, I knew you'd think I'd done it on purpose to trap you. Asking you to marry me, was my desperate attempt to keep you and my baby, I couldn't face the thought of being a single mother, I knew I'd never be able to cope alone.'

'You killed our baby without even consulting me?' Simon stared at Laura in horrified realisation.

Laura paled, and went very still, her eyes locked with his. 'It's what you said you wanted.'

'I was young and stupid, I never thought it would apply to us. You should have told me Laura, given me a chance. I can't believe you made that decision by yourself. It was wrong and selfish, I thought better of you, Laura.'

'Yes, well,' Laura stood up sharply, pushing her chair away. 'It seems we were both wrong about a lot of things. Goodbye, Simon, hopefully this time forever. Charles, it will probably take me a couple of weeks to calm down and forgive you, so I suggest you don't call me for at least that long. Goodbye, everyone, it was nice to have met you, I hope you all enjoyed the entertaining spectacle of watching two people, who should have known better, washing their dirty laundry in public.'

'Laura...' Charles half stood, in a vain attempt to stop her, but she had already fled from the room, closing the door forcibly behind her.

'Magnificent,' breathed the opera singer.

'She sure is one feisty little lady,' drawled the comedian.

'What passion, what heart,' the opera singer continued. She looked sharply at Simon. 'It is obvious, she still loves you very much, are you simply going to let her walk out of your life again, or are you going to go after her?'

'Go after her? But, you heard her, she killed our baby. I don't think I can ever forgive her for that.'

'Men!' exclaimed the opera singer, rolling her eyes in disgust. 'Are you all born stupid, or simply practice hard at being so dense? I did not hear her say any such thing,' she broke off, looked slyly at Charles. 'Are you going to tell him, or shall I?'

'Tell me what?' Simon's voice had the desperate edge of a man who was rapidly losing control. 'Charles?'

'Laura has a child,' Charles paused, enjoying the dramatic moment, savouring it. 'A little girl, she is coming up to her tenth birthday.'

'A daughter? I have a daughter?' Simon gazed around the table in bewildered consternation. 'A daughter!' A grin spread across his face. 'I have a daughter? My god, I have a daughter!' He was laughing now, the other guests smiling with him. 'Oh, my god, Laura! I have to go, thank you, Charles, goodbye.'

A relieved cheer broke out around the table, as Simon too jumped up, knocking over his chair, and raced out of the room.

'Will he catch her, do you think?' enquired the politician.

'Oh yes,' smiled the diva. 'I do not think she will be walking very fast.'

Charles prided himself on hosting excellent dinner parties, but surpassed himself, with the one he held in honour of that delightfully attractive couple, Simon and Laura Mills, upon their return from honeymoon.

The End...

The Fat Club

There are three of us. Me, Jan and Mo, all new girls.
We watch the easy familiarity of the others,
Those who joined in the usual post-Christmas rush,
During the fatly depressing month of January,
When resolutions have been decisively made,
And, just as decisively, broken.

Now we sit, in a row, in a cheerless, church hall,
On a cold, wet night in March.
Three silent, uncertain, newcomers.
We eye each other, wondering, assessing,
Before Mo breaks the ice, names are exchanged,
We share, reasons...excuses...hopes...expectations.

Mine is sudden realisation what months of comfort eating,
Binging to forget the pain of a nowhere marriage,
Have done to a once slender frame.
Now I want to reclaim, rediscover, reaffirm, my existence.

Jan wants to lose weight for her daughter's wedding,
She's already bought the suit, she explains, breathlessly,
In a size too small, deliberately so,
She will...must...drop at least a dress size, or two, or else...
The else is left hanging, her fear of failure a living thing.

As for Mo, well, she's there to lose her baby fat.
Many weeks pass, before I learn, her youngest is 21,
Baby fat, come of age.

We meet, each and every Tuesday, come rain or shine.
To trade our successes and our failures.
To encourage, congratulate, commiserate.
Jan loses steadily, a comfortable two pounds a week.
Plodding, predictable, her smug satisfaction growing.

I lose unpredictably, a miserly pound one week,
Then an awe inspiring seven the next. Recently acquired,
My bulk dissipates as quickly as it came,
But then, as I'm frequently reminded, I'm the lucky one,
The young one, the single one. The one who can,
Fill her fridge with Perrier, smoked salmon and salad.
Can have empty cupboards, the one with no husband
To complain, no children to moan.

Mo treads water, lose a pound, gain two.
Her shiny cheeks crinkling at each disappointment,
Inviting us to join in her self-ridiculing. And we do,
She is our clown, our court jester, and so, we laugh.
Once, face deadly earnest, she claims to be anorexic,
And we gaze, dumb struck, at bones buried
Beneath layers of flesh, rippling, rolling,
Mountains of body, bulging through clothes,
Spilling over shoes, tightening under a wedding ring,
Until it has to be cut off, from a finger oozing with pain.
Gently, the leader asks the question we are all thinking,
And Mo blinks innocently, because, she explains,
Every time I look in the mirror, I see a fat woman.
The room explodes, the class clown has entertained us.

Jan's daughter gets married. She wears her suit with pride.
I achieve my goal. Weight lost, and more beside.
Gradually, life becomes busy, crammed with the pursuits
Of the very thin, the very young, the very single.
I stop going. Years pass.
The Fat Club relegated to shady recesses of memory.
Something to be, if not ashamed about, at least, silent of.

Then, unexpectedly, I bump into Jan.
Buying treats for her grandchildren, she displays
Obligatory photos, to which I make the right noises,
Before asking, innocently, if she has seen
Anything lately of Mo?
At once, her glow fades, her expression becomes somber,
Her hand clutches my arm. Didn't I know?
She asks. Hadn't I heard?

She tells me a tale, of a late-night call to the ambulance,
Of frantic attempts, of stomach pumps,
And medical intervention, all to no avail.
Mo, that class clown, that court jester,
In reality, so desperate, so unhappy, life became too much,
Too hard, too difficult, to endure any longer.

Guilt, rank and cloying, grips my throat.
A guilt that still lingers, recognising I should have,
Could have, would have, noticed her need, her pain,
If only I'd not been too young, too ignorant, too selfish.
The concern I felt now, too little, too late,
To make a difference.

Friendship

As tough as twisted steel,
As fragile as spun sugar.
The gift you gave was special, precious.
But, in a stupid, careless, moment,
I broke it.
Shattered it, so completely,
No repair was possible.
So, you took it back.

Do You

Believe?

**Susan was never one for flights of fancy, so
what is she to think when her daughter tells
her a fairy has taken up residence at the
bottom of the garden**

Do You Believe?

'Mummy, a fairy's moved into our garden.'

'Has it, dear? That's nice,' Susan Clarke delivered the standard answer, mind on other things, as she dished up her small daughter's dinner, and helped her into her chair.

'Yes, she's moved into the biggest of the bird houses daddy made.'

Susan frowned, Jessica's words reminding her of the row she'd had with Neil that morning, about those very same bird houses.

A skilled carpenter, her husband, Neil, had painstakingly made the beautiful bird houses in his spare time, each one an exact replica of the houses in their close. Although, Susan admired his talent, the workmanship involved, she'd been disbelieving, cutting in her condemnation he was seriously considering giving up his job – his stable, well paid, job – in order to start his own business as a carpenter.

'Please, Sue,' he'd pleaded, his tone reasonable. 'I know I can do this, I'm good enough, and there's definitely a market for well crafted, bespoke, pieces, especially with the internet, I could even sell world-wide.'

'What about your job?' she'd demanded, fear making her voice shrill.

'I hate my job,' he'd paused, his expression weary. 'Let's face it, Sue, I'm not cut out to be a nine to five businessman, I've stuck it this long because of the money, but, with each week that goes by, I'm more and more unhappy...'

'Unhappy?' she'd interrupted bitterly. 'Well, if you put your own personal happiness, above that of your wife and child.'

'That's not fair, Sue, and you know it,' he'd retaliated. 'I've worked long and hard to gain security for us. The mortgage is paid off, there's savings in the bank, now is a good time to break free, to stop doing something I hate and start doing something I love!'

She'd turned away from him, tears pricking her eyes, heart hammering with fear he was seriously considering jeopardizing their future, their security, on a selfish whim.

'Sue, please...'

She'd stayed silent, turned her face resolutely away from him. Eventually, he'd sighed and left for work.

Now, her mind lingered on the scene. Had she been too harsh, too critical? Would it not have been better to sit down and listen to his plans, at least appear to consider the matter from all angles? Then, calmly and logically, point out the flaws, so the whole silly notion could be dismissed and forgotten about.

Jessica stuck a fork into her mashed potato, mulched it into a pile, her face thoughtful.

'The fairy says she's come to warn us, she said something terrible is going to happen, and that she wants to help us.'

'Something terrible?' Startled out of her thoughts, Susan stared back at five-year-old Jessica's solemn little face. 'Whatever are you talking about, darling?'

'The fairy,' persisted Jessica. 'She said something bad is coming.'

'What sort of something bad?' Susan asked, well used to Jessica's games of make believe, she was, nonetheless, surprised at the dark tinge to this particular fantasy. Normally, Jessica's imaginings involved happy, talking, animals and multi coloured unicorns.

'She said she wasn't sure,' Jessica put her head to one side, nose wrinkling, as if trying to remember. 'Fairies never know for definite, they can't see into the future exactly, you know,' she informed her mother, knowledgeably. 'They just know if something bad or good is going to happen.'

'I see,' replied her mother. 'Well, never mind, eat your dinner now, it's getting late.'

Jessica surveyed her plate with disapproval, pushed at the carrots, looking guiltily at her mother, as some dropped from her plate onto the table.

'Really, Jess,' Susan began, her patience fraying at the edges, then stopped. Behind her, the phone began to ring. And an inexplicable, cold, dread gripped her heart...

An hour later, Jessica's words echoed through her mind, as she stood by the side of the hospital bed and stared at Neil's still, white, face. Unable to believe, to comprehend, she gazed blindly at tubes snaking from his body, to a machine whose persistent beeps showed he was, thankfully, still alive.

Desperately, she turned to the doctor, clutched his white sleeve, hungry for reassurance.

'He's going to be alright, isn't he, doctor? I mean...he will get better, won't he?'

'It's hard to say,' the doctor's eyes softened, sympathetically. 'His head took a hard knock in the accident, there's swelling in the brain, and he's showed no signs of waking from the coma. Until he does, we can have no way of knowing how extensive the damage is to his brain.'

'Brain damage?' Susan's voice faltered. She stuffed her knuckles into her mouth, throat closing in panic. Brain damage – no, not Neil, not her wonderful, clever, Neil!

Explaining to Jessica, was the hardest thing Susan had ever done in her life. Unable to speak, she simply held her daughter's slight body as she cried, and it was over an hour before Jessica lay, drained and limp, in her arms, and Susan was able to carry her up to bed.

'Mummy?'

'Yes, sweetheart?'

'Is this the something terrible, the fairy said was going to happen?'

Susan was still for a moment, then slowly nodded. Fresh tears scorched her eyes, and she hoped her daughter would not see them in the dimness of the nightlight.

'I think it must be,' Jessica answered her own question. 'Because, I can't think of anything worse than this, can you, mummy?'

Susan remained silent. She could think of something far worse, felt sick to her soul at the thought of losing Neil, bitter guilt welling, every time she remembered the quarrel, and her spiteful, cruel, words.

Days crawled past. Family and friends rallied round, looking after Jessica during the long hours Susan spent by Neil's bedside. Hopefully, she scrutinised her husband's still face, praying for his eyes to open, for a flicker of movement, for any sign of life at all.

Gently, the doctor explained, how each day he stayed in a coma gave greater cause for concern. After a week, Susan began to despair, to consider the awful possibility Neil would never wake up, would never come home, and an icy fist slowly closed about her heart.

'Mummy, the fairy's hungry. Can we make her a cake?' About to snap out a curt negative, something in her daughter's eyes stopped her, and Susan bit her lip, angry with herself for wanting to take her secret fears out on Jessica. Quietly, she hugged her, long and hard, realising she'd been neglecting her daughter during the endless days, suddenly understanding, Jessica was scared and lonely too.

'Yes,' she agreed. 'I think that's a lovely idea, you go and get our aprons, I'll look out my recipe for fairy cakes. You can even put sprinkles on them, if you like.

Later, as Jessica carefully carried the plate of haphazardly decorated cakes to the bottom of the garden to share with the fairy, Susan watched her go from the kitchen door, wondering if this fancy about the fairy was Jessica's way of coping with what had happened.

Here, Susan's thoughts paused and she frowned, but, hadn't Jessica mentioned the fairy before the accident?

'Did she like the cakes?' Susan asked, when Jessica finally came back with the empty plate, crumbs and sugar icing clinging to her face and clothes.

'Yes, but she only ate one because she's so small,' Jessica paused, then put her head on one side and surveyed her mother thoughtfully. 'Mummy, what's a sinicall?'

'A sinicall?' Susan asked in confusion. 'Whatever do you mean, darling?'

'Well, the fairy says she can't help us because you're too sinicall. She says your heart is all shriveled, that you don't believe in anything, and unless you believe in something, she can't help.'

'Oh, you mean cynical,' Susan stared at Jessica. 'Well, a cynic never sees the good side of life, they always think negatively. But, that's not me. I'm not a cynic...'

'Yes, you are, mummy,' Jessica insisted, with the brutal honesty of the very young. 'You always think things are going to go wrong, you never believe in nice things.'

Stunned speechless, Susan sat down heavily in a chair, stung by the ring of truth in her daughter's words.

'The fairy said that believing releases good endo...somethings, into the atmosphere, and that's what keeps fairies alive. She says there aren't many fairies left now, because even children don't believe in them anymore. But I believe, that's why she came here, and daddy believes, so she wanted to help us. But, now the bad thing has happened and it happened to daddy, and she says there's not enough of those good endomorphy things here, so she can't help.'

Long after Jessica was in bed and asleep, Susan roamed the house, unable to settle, her daughter's words resounding in her brain.

Was she a cynic? Did she always look for the bad in life, never see the good? No, surely not, but a small, niggling, voice whispered maybe Jess, and the fairy, were right. When was the last time she'd believed in anything? She remembered all the times she'd shaken her head in exasperation, when Neil and Jess played their games of make-believe.

'Stop filling her head with nonsense,' she'd told him, and he'd laughed at her.

'Everyone should have a little fantasy in their lives,' he'd insisted. 'We all need to believe in something, it's not healthy to be so cynical.'

That word again, she'd forgotten, until now, Neil called her that too.

On a whim, Susan went into the spare room. It was dark, but a full moon shone brightly through the bare window, allowing her to see almost to the bottom of the garden. Pressing her hot forehead against the cool glass, she strained her eyes to make out the bird houses, hanging in the dark shadows of the little cluster of trees by the back fence.

For almost an hour she stood, the dark stillness of the room pressing onto her eardrums, listening to the night time sounds of the sleeping house. She waited, but waited for what, she couldn't say.

Should she have supported Neil in his desire to start his own business? After all, he was right, financially they were secure enough to withstand a few lean times. An image flashed into her mind of Neil's drawn, exhausted, face every evening after work; of how different he was in his studio, where he spent hours lovingly working the wood.

If she believed in just one thing, she believed in her husband, in his abilities. She also knew, if he ever thought his family's future was uncertain, he was not the type to blindly follow his dream, no, he'd give up, go back to paid employment.

Susan bowed her head in shamed realisation. She'd been wrong, selfish, so wrapped up in her own desperate need for security, she'd completely failed to consider her husband's needs.

'I do believe,' she softly whispered. 'Oh, Neil, I believe in you, I believe in us.'

Suddenly, it felt as if an iron band had been released from around her heart, to allow hope to creep softly inside. Blinking back tears, she gazed blindly out into the dark garden and saw it.

A light – soft, pink, glowing - it appeared where she knew the biggest bird house hung. Brightly, it flared, then flittered up through the trees and was gone. For long minutes she stood, hoping it would come back, wondering what it had been

Her heart then jumped with shock, as behind her, in the still house, the phone began to ring.

'It's a miracle,' declared the doctor. 'Mind you, they do happen sometimes.' Susan nodded, unable to release her husband's hand or tear her eyes away from his, the tears sliding unashamedly down her cheeks.

'I was so worried,' she finally murmured. 'When you wouldn't wake up, I thought...'

'You thought the worse,' he finished, grinning ruefully. 'That's my Sue.'

'No, no,' she hurried to correct him. 'You're wrong, I've changed, I do believe now, I do. I think you should give up your job, I believe you'll make a real success of being a carpenter, and you're right, you should be happy.'

'My word,' he said, his eyes crinkling in confusion. 'What brought about this change of heart?

'I realised, there is something I believe in,' she replied. 'Something I believe in more than anything. I believe in you.'

The End...

This is Heaven

Where the birds sing, and the bees hum,
And the afternoon sun catches and stays,
Baking paths and metal chairs,
Until they bite at unwary flesh.
Where I learn how to breathe again.
Where she creates, a fantasy land,
A world peopled with little folk.
Where flowers nod, and blossom drifts
From an over fertile cherry tree,
Thick with promise of dark, sweet, fruits to come,
The delights of jam, pies and cherry brandy.
Here, now, this is heaven.

A red tin watering can, inexpertly plied
As she waters with careless abandon,
Plants, lawn, paths and feet, all thoroughly soaked.
A slumbering cat, bonelessly sprawled in a plant pot,
Flecks of sun hardened soil sprinkling its soft belly fur.
An indignant, shocked, protest,
As it too is watered, in hopes it may grow.
An Englishman's home, may be his castle,
But for this Englishwoman, it is her garden.
This tiny, non-descript plot of land,
Bound on all sides by house and fence,
Yet, look up, look up, above is ten thousand acres of sky.

A bowlful of water for the making of mud pies,
Long grass for a jungle, home to so many animals,
That, on the rare occasions I mow,
A thorough search must be mounted,
To ensure no loss of plastic life.
I am reliably informed, fairies inhabit our garden.
Drawn by its disordered unruliness, its wild abandon.
And, sometimes, eyes half closed against the sun,
Senses tuned into the busy thrum of nature,
I fancy I see them, quick and jewel like,
Darting and weaving,

Their wings incandescent blurs of movement.

She makes a snail farm.
Suppressing shudders, I watch, as she searches
Dark, secret places for livestock,
Confidently plucking each up by its shell,
Displaying green frilly underskirt. Delighting,
When one ventures probing horns from its tawny home.
She finds a green beetle, carapace hexagonal.
Watching, for what seems hours, its patient scrambling,
Over the obstacle course she's built for its amusement,
And I sympathise with its frustration,
Its forever climbing of twigs and leaves,
Antennae vibrating in questioning bafflement,
It scurries in endless circles,
Before she finally grows bored, and sets it free.

I'm given cups of delicious mud tea,
My plate piled high with gourmet delights
Such as twig soup and dandelion cake,
Which I eat, with appreciative relish,
Until she is satisfied, and I can return, with relief,
To my glass of Chardonnay, droplets of cold condense on
My palm, the shock of icy tartness on my tongue,
I tip my head back, eyes shut,
Feel the caress of sun, warm on my face.
Where time stands still; and an afternoon lasts forever,
Where a child can imagine; and an adult forget.
Where secrets are whispered; and promises made.
Here, now, this is heaven.

The Race

You can't catch me,
Cried the child, and ran.
Laughter erupting in great,
Knicker wetting, gulps.

Catch me if you can,
Taunted the teenager.
Eyes heavy with promise,
The power of youth.

We must catch up,
Cooed the career woman.
Insincerity via an iPhone,
Brain busy multitasking.

Wish I could just catch up,
Moaned the mother.
Dreams buried under duty,
Hopes strangled by birth.

You've caught me,
Groaned the grandmother.
Sagging with loser's defeat,
An un-winnable race, now over.

Vicious

Circle

As far as DI Cass Sawyer is concerned, the past should remain firmly in the past, but it seems time may have different plans

Vicious Circle

Some days, have the capacity to just really piss me off. Like today, with my car in the garage having its cam belt replaced, I could have done without it raining, but rain it did. Continuous miserable, really wet, rain, that leaked, non-stop, from the sky for the whole day, making my hair frizz. God, I hate that, DI Cass Sawyer, tough, ballsy, no nonsense woman, trying to make it in a man's world, looking like an extra from the Muppet Show.

Upon finally arriving home, desperate for a very cold glass of Chardonnay, a very hot shower and a plate of something in front of mindless TV; I found that Greg, the latest in a not so long line of men, dumb enough to try the doomed-to-failure experiment of living with me; had finally cracked and moved out, leaving a note stuck to the fridge by way of explanation.

'Dear Cass,' I read. 'I'm sorry, but I can't do this anymore. A relationship is supposed to be two-way, and, even though I love you, I can't go on giving and receiving nothing in return, Greg. PS. I would have spoken to you in person, but, once again, you're late home.'

Late? Was I so very late? A glance at the kitchen clock agreed that, at nearly 10pm, yes, I was late. He had me there. A further memory stirred, something about promising to be home for dinner, that he needed to 'talk'. He wasn't being fair though, a break had come in a case and I'd had to...shit, let's be honest, I'd had to nothing,

nothing that couldn't have waited till morning anyway. I was only crawling through the door at this sorry excuse of a time, because I'd not wanted to talk, had known, deep down, precisely what he'd wanted to talk about.

Damn, damn, damn, I'd really liked this one as well, had even begun to think that, maybe, he was the one man I could finally open up to and trust.

I so definitely needed that wine now, but quickly discovered, as well as removing himself from my flat, the bastard hadn't been shopping either. I suppose it was unfair of me to complain; but complain I did, loudly and voraciously, with a little bit of door slamming thrown in for good measure.

It made me feel marginally better, but didn't alter the fact that, other than dried pasta and a bottle of seriously out of date orange squash, I had absolutely nothing in the flat to eat or drink. There was nothing for it; I was going to have to go out again.

I looked out the window, at the dark, unwelcoming, weather lashing against the glass and inwardly groaned, wondering if maybe I could hold on till tomorrow, but a prolonged and noisy stomach grumble soon put paid to that idea. I was starving, had had nothing, other than a dodgy sausage roll nicked from my sergeant, all day.

'Fuck,' I muttered, some days really did piss me off.

Letting myself back out, there was a sudden explosion of noise from the bushes, and the most pitiful example of cathood slunk out, keeping his distance, and eyeing me balefully with a malevolent orange glare.

'Hey Roadkill, sorry, no food for either of us, until I've been to the shops.' A string of feline shrieks and curses followed this comment, and I hastily removed myself from his launch trajectory.

Roadkill is a stray whom I feed from time to time, but this doesn't seem to have won me a place in his affections, or lessened his mistrust of me. Indeed, it's been made plain to me that any attempt to touch or, heaven forbid, pet him, will result in a serious mauling.

As I sympathise with such a fierce desire to be left alone, a grudging sort of respect has sprung up between us. I pause at the end of the path and look back at him.

'I'll bring you back something to eat, I promise.' The feral cat simply stared at me, unblinking. 'Salmon, maybe,' I wheedled. Roadkill, supremely unimpressed, gave a feline shrug and skulked back under the bushes.

Heading down the road, I suddenly realise, because I have no car, I have to make a decision as to which route to take. To reach the only late-night opening shop in the area, it's about twenty minutes by car, but double that on foot. There's a short cut through the park, but I never go that way, because, if I do, I'll have to pass the old Smithson house.

Nobody knows why it's called that, maybe, sometime in the distant past, a family called Smithson lived there, but it's been standing empty, slowly disintegrating for at least the past 40 years. It's a huge monstrosity of a place and I hate it. I never go past it, never. I won't even go into the park; the house affects me that much.

I remember, last summer, Greg prepared a surprise picnic for us to have in the park. His confused expression as I flatly refused to go, which slowly turned to anger when I could offer no explanation as to why not. My eyes prickle, and I scrub at them impatiently. I will not let myself feel, simply because yet another man has walked out on me.

God, I really, really need that drink now, and my stomach sounds like it's given up and has begun eating my internal organs. If I take the longer route it's going to be nearly two hours before I'm home again, whereas, going through the park will cut it down to one, still I hesitate at the park entrance, every nerve ending screaming at me to turn back.

'This is ridiculous, Cass!' I say to myself firmly, and march into the park. At that hour, it's deserted, and I hunch further into my jacket, as rain drips from the trees and wind blows a cold, damp, squall into my face.

The moon briefly sails from behind dark, looming, clouds, tree branches rustle violently in the wind, my own heart thuds painfully in my ear. In short, I am in the middle of a fricking horror movie, all it needs is for an eerie howl to suddenly start up and the whole picture will be complete.

Trying not to think of another night, just as dark and stormy as this, the night it...Yanking firmly on the memory before it can even think about going there, I brace myself, mentally running through what I need to buy, force my reluctant feet to step on and on, until, suddenly, I turn a corner and there it is.

It's funny, but it doesn't seem as big or as menacing as I remember. Maybe, over the years, I've built it up to monstrous proportions in my mind, but, seeing it again through adult eyes, it seems diminished, rather pathetic really.

'Tragic, what happened there, wasn't it?' I jump, heart pounding painfully at my rib cage. A dog walker has appeared out of the dark to stand beside me, gazing up at the house. A drenched, elderly, corgi, that looks as pissed off as I feel, squats in damp, mute, misery at the end of a lead.

I make a non-committal noise, wanting him to stop talking and go away. I stare at the house, clenching my teeth so firmly, a nerve pops in my temple. It's just a house, just a house, just a...oh fuck!

'I expect you know all about it?' he pauses, takes my silence as an invitation to continue. 'It happened about twenty years ago, a young girl was snatched from the local children's home that used to be over there,' he vaguely gestures towards the east, and my eyes follow his hand, my face numb.

'By one of those mental patients they keep releasing from hospital, you know,' he continues, oblivious to my frozen stare. 'Care in the community, and all that bollocks,' he actually nudges me in the ribs. In my head, I knock him to the ground and kick him into silence; in reality, I merely wince away.

'Care in the community,' he says again and snorts, leaving me in no doubt as to his feelings on the matter. 'Anyway, he took her and kept her in this house for days, doing God knows what to her, before slitting his own throat.' He shook his head in vicarious, ghoulish, appreciation. 'Shocking, hey?'

He blinked at me, glasses misted by the rain, then, seemingly disappointed by my lack of response, he pulls his dog to its feet and they wander off, him still shaking his head and casting sidelong glances at the house, the dog with its tail firmly between its legs.

I'm left, standing alone, rooted to the spot, unable to take my eyes off the house, battling the heady surge of memories. It had been three days he'd held the girl prisoner, I know, because I can still remember every single pain and terror filled second of them.

Seventy-two long hours, during which every indignity imaginable had been inflicted upon my ten-year-old body by a man whom, by rights, should never have been walking the streets.

What he did to me...I start to shake, fuck! fuck! fuck! I will not allow this to happen, not now, not here, not ever. For twenty years, I'd successfully suppressed it, treading on it firmly, every time it tried to make me remember, to think about what he...

It's no use, the memories scream at me, and I remember going down to the kitchen of the children's home for a glass of water, unlocking the door to look at the rain, why, why had I done that? Stupid, stupid child!

I knew why, the others had been bullying me, again. I'd unlocked the door, because the urge to run was so strong. I'd never thought about any danger there might be, all I'd done was unlock the door, that was all. But, I'd let him in.

I swallowed hard, bile rising, as I remembered the heart stopping terror when he'd grabbed me, that split second when I could have screamed, but, was so scared, I couldn't, then he'd taped my mouth, slung me over his shoulder like an old carpet or something.

Rain was dripping down the neck of my jacket as I stood there, unable to do anything to stop the riptide of memories flooding through my brain. In twenty years, I'd never allowed myself to remember, instead locked them in a box and thrown away the key. Well, they were hammering to be let out now.

I remembered, many years ago, soon after I became a sergeant, looking up the police report on the incident, seeking answers, but instead finding only confusion and mystery. Who had alerted the police to my whereabouts?

The report stated the police had received an anonymous tip off over the telephone, and that a single, young, uniform, had been dispatched to investigate what was deemed to be a hoax call.

What he'd found, instead, was a truly horrific scene; a young girl, sitting at the top of the stairs, drenched in blood, sobbing uncontrollably in the arms of a strange woman. A woman whose cool, professional, manner and steely gaze, had the uniform instantly snapping to attention, and accepting, without question, her assumption of authority.

In the room beyond had been the stuff of nightmares, vivid, scarlet, arterial, blood splattered across almost every surface. The body, slumped on the floor, knife still clasped in hand. The naïve uniform had taken one look at his first dead body, swallowed down his vomit, and speedily agreed to take the victim back to the station, where a social worker would be summoned and parents, if any, alerted, leaving the DI at the scene to await the arrival of the SOCO team.

I remembered my stunned disbelief, as I'd read the report. Who was that woman? If not a real DI, then what was she? Where had she come from and where did she disappear to? Not less than ten minutes after the uniform had taken me from the house, the SOCO team had arrived to find no DI, real or otherwise, waiting for them and no evidence that she'd ever existed at all; other than a sketchy report from an inexperienced uniform, and the ramblings of a traumatised ten-year-old child.

Over the years, I'd tried hard to sharpen my memories of her, but, the only image I'd retained, was a hazy one of a tall, rangy, woman with short, tousled, hair and kind eyes. She'd taken me from that room, where I'd witnessed my abuser's suicide, sat with me on the top of the stairs and, with a few calm, steady, words, had pulled me back from a complete breakdown.

I'd long considered her my mentor, my inspiration, the reason why I myself had joined the police force. I think, I'd even harboured the never-voiced hope, I would one day meet her again. You can imagine my shock, when I discovered nobody knew who she was.

The rain had increased, lashing against the trees, spitting coldness into my face. A chill wind gusted through the park, rattling dead leaves in front of it like dispossessed souls. It's time to go, too much time has been wasted on the past. Although, I feel a certain satisfaction I have successfully faced my demons, I'm cold, wet and hungry. I need food, I need warmth, I need to cry.

Casting one last look up at the old house, I turn to leave, and a high-pitched scream splits the night. I freeze, the thought flashing across my mind perhaps my triggering of old, long suppressed, memories, has caused me to imagine it. No, there it is again! Not so piercing this time, but still, panic packed, and it definitely came from inside the house.

Terror stabs at my gut. I really, really don't want to go in there. Know I must. Rain, or is it tears, chills my face with fingers of icy fear. I listen for another scream. Silence. Even more terrifying than the screams, I strain my ears to listen to it, the hairs creeping into individual life on my head. Seconds pass like eons, then I hear it, a wild, desperate, sobbing.

Reluctantly, one foot dragging behind the other, I stumble up the weed choked path, pushing open the old, rotting, gate and stepping into the shambolic, overgrown, garden. As I pass through the gate, a wave of nausea catches me unawares and I nearly fall, clutching desperately at a gatepost to steady myself.

Blinking frantically to clear my suddenly blurry vision, I stagger up the path towards the front door. The crying abruptly stops. For some reason, this unnerves me even more, and I pause on the doorstep, feeling an icy shiver run down my spine.

Groping blindly in my pocket, I draw out my mobile, hit speed dial for the station, curse impatiently as it struggles to connect, then begin talking almost as soon as it's answered.

'This is DI Cass Sawyer requesting immediate backup at the old Smithson property in the park.'

There's silence for a moment, before a crackly voice says. 'Who? I'm sorry, DI who?'

'DI Cass Sawyer,' I snap, cursing my bad luck to have got some idiot, new guy, who didn't know who I was.

'I'm sorry, Miss, but we have no DI Sawyer currently at this station. Are you sure you've phoned the right number?'

'Who the fuck is this?' I demand impatiently.

'This is Sergeant Wilkins, and I'll thank you not to speak to me like that, Miss.'

'Well listen up, Sergeant Wilkins! You claim never to have heard of me, unfortunately, I've now heard of you, and by the time I'm through with you, you'll wish I hadn't! Now, get backup to the old Smithson property in the park immediately!'

I cut off his outraged squawks, shoved the phone in my pocket and considered my options. I could wait for backup, or go in by myself. It took less than thirty seconds for me to decide. I was going in.

Taking a deep breath, I pushed on the door, and managed to force it open just far enough for me to slip through. Once inside, I struggled to clamp down the waves of dread and panic welling up inside; nothing has changed, it still looks exactly the way it did twenty years ago.

Silently, I creep up the stairs, feeling the invisible cord pulling me up, towards that room. Hearing no sound but the thudding of my own heart, I reach the top of the stairs, cross the landing, softly turn the door handle and ease it open.

I see the body first, crumpled in the centre of the room like a pile of old, dirty laundry; and then the blood, good god, how much blood was there? It had splashed onto every surface, even the ceiling. I didn't need to examine the body to establish the cause of death, he'd obviously slit his own throat, just like...quickly, I pushed the thought away and turned to survey the rest of the room.

Oh, fucking hell, she was huddled in the corner behind the door, well, as far into the corner as she'd been able to get. I saw, with total disbelief, the manacle around her skinny ankle, the flesh beneath bruised and torn, the chain that reached a short distance to an iron ring driven fast into the solid wood skirting board.

Just like me. Just like he'd done to me. I swallowed down the guilt, copycat crime, not my fault...not my fault. Blame it on the sick bastard now lying in a pool of his own blood.

Softly, I approached, she scrunched away, petrified, absolute terror oozing from every pore. I knelt beside her, Christ, how young she was, so very young, but with a look in her eyes that told me she'd left childhood far behind.

'Come on, honey,' I said gently, desperately trying to remember what my saviour had said to me, all those years ago, what words she'd used to pull me back.

'He's dead,' the voice was flat, emotionless.

'That's right, he is,' I agreed.

She looked at me, madness nibbling at the corner of her vision, and I flinched inside, so much damage in one so young.

'What he did to me...' she started to shake, the enormity of it all over-riding her emotions. 'He...' she yelped, 'he...' she wiped a grimy hand caked with blood – hers, his? – over her eyes. 'He hurt me,' she finished in a whisper, and I felt my heart break at the simple, awful, words.

'I know,' I murmured. 'I know he did, but he can never hurt you again.' She glanced wildly at me, her eyes flicking back to the bag of bones on the floor, then she nodded, just once, sharp and decisive.

Cautiously, I stood, looking around the room, saw a small table in the corner furthest from the girl. On it some food remains, tins of beer, a key...thank god, I grabbed it, approached her too fast, she started back, manacle biting at her tender flesh.

'Sorry,' I cried, as she gasped in renewed pain. I held up the key, 'let's see if this fits, shall we?' I murmured, trying to keep my voice low and my movements calm.

I waited, until she nodded, head down on her knees, her thin arms wrapped protectively around her body. Taking it as permission, I knelt down, tried the key in the manacle lock, it fitted, the heavy band falling from her ankle with a thud.

She flexed her ankle, her relief evident.

'Let me take you out of here,' I offered. She considered, then slowly held up a hand. Gently, I eased her up off the floor, supporting her, helped her hobble from the room, turning her body away from the mess on the floor.

She made it to the top of the stairs, then slid down me, collapsing in a heap on the step, clutching at the post, banging her head as she rocked, keening out her pain.

'Why?' she sobbed, as I hastily sat beside her and cupped my hand around her head to protect it. 'Why? Why did he...'

Take me, rape me, hurt me, destroy me...I finish the sentence in my head, yet remain silent.

'Why?' she looks at me, pleading for an answer, and my heart aches for her; for the suffering she has yet to come, as the memories echo down the years, stunting her emotional growth, never allowing her to truly trust or love. I shift uncomfortably on the step, in a nutshell, exactly what has happened to me.

Suddenly, she turns to me, buries her head in my shoulder and begins to cry; deep, soul wrenching, sobs. I hold her close and gently rock her, murmuring soft, soothing, words.

'Anyone here?' I feel her tense in my arms, and look down as a young, uniformed, officer pokes his head through the door and looks around.

'Up here.' He mounts the stairs, eyes widening as he takes in the blood stained, half naked, girl weeping softly in my arms.

'DI Cass Sawyer,' I state crisply. 'And you are?'

'Collins, ma'am,' he seems relieved that someone in authority is here. 'What appears to be the situation ma'am?'

'The situation, Collins, is there's a dead body in that room, and a young lady here in need of medical attention and her parents.'

'Dead body?' he swallows, casts a quick, nervous glance at the door. 'Should I...?'

'By all means, go and take a look,' I reply, amused by his unease, at the same time, intrigued by his uniform. What was it that seemed wrong about it? 'Just don't touch anything.'

He nods, crosses the landing and enters the room. A moment later he's back, swallowing violently, looking decidedly green about the gills, sweat breaking out on his naïve face.

'Is your vehicle outside, Collins?'

'Yes, ma'am.'

'Good. I want you to take this young lady back to the station; radio ahead to make sure a social worker is called in, and request a SOCO team be sent to this location immediately. I'll wait here for them, and check that nothing is disturbed.' Gently, I help her to her feet, attempt to pass her over to Collins.

'No,' she clutches at me with a strength born of

desperation. 'Don't leave me!' she begs. 'Please, I want to stay with you.'

'Ssh, it's ok, honey,' I soothe. 'Collins is going to take you back to the station. I have to stay here for a little while, and then I promise I'll come and find you, I promise, I won't leave you alone.'

With much reassurance, I finally manage to persuade her to go with Collins, and settle down to await the arrival of the SOCO team, my mind in turmoil, as I think about the way history has repeated itself here tonight.

I hope she'll cope with the experience better than I have; because I can see now I haven't coped at all. Not really. Instead, I've bottled it up, hidden it so deep there's no escaping it. I've allowed myself to become so rooted in my fears of the past, it's stopped me from living in the present.

Emotionally, I am still that traumatised ten-year-old, unable to comprehend men could ever be anything but the enemy, givers of pain, not to be trusted.

No wonder I had problems forming adult relationships, no wonder Greg had left me. No wonder they'd all left me, As I sit there, in that house of death and horror, I feel the old hurts loosen their grip. Maybe, it was possible I could move on from that point, no longer be a prisoner of my own fears. At least now, I knew I wanted to try.

I stood up and paced the hall checking my watch. Where the hell was the SOCO team? Collins had left over half an hour ago; they should have been here by now. Impatiently, I pull out my mobile, no signal, with a muttered curse I step back through the front door and try again, still no signal, fuming, I stomp all over the weeds in the front garden, banging through the decrepit gate.

Nausea, sudden and intense, brought me to my knees, spitting out the rank taste of bile and an empty stomach, bugger, I knew that sausage roll had been dodgy.

Staggering back up, I see I have bars and speed dial the station, this time a familiar voice answers.

'Phillips? It's DI Sawyer here. Where the hell is that SOCO team I requested?'

'SOCO team ma'am?' It was obvious from the confusion in his voice, this is the first Phillips has heard of it.

'Hasn't Collins made it back yet?'

'Collins, ma'am? I don't believe we have anyone called Collins here. Shall I go and check on that SOCO team for you, ma'am?'

I'm just about to say yes, when I notice something strange. When I'd comforted the girl, some of the blood splattered on her had transferred itself to my clothes and hands, but now, looking down at myself, I see, to my surprise, there's no trace of blood on me at all.

I frown, leaning on the gatepost, check the soles of my shoes, I'd walked right through a puddle of blood...but they're clean, apart from mud from the garden, no blood at all. I frown.

'Ma'am? Are you still there? Is everything alright?'

'It's alright, Phillips.' I slowly reply, things suddenly tumbling into place to make a strange, impossible, sort of sense. 'My mistake, don't worry about it.'

'Yes, ma'am.' From his tone, it's plain he thinks I've completely lost it, will probably lose no time informing the whole station, but I'll worry about that later.

I disconnect the phone, slowly re-enter the house. Climbing the stairs again, I go through my few memories of the woman who'd taken me from that room; her short, tousled, hair – absently, I run a hand through my own cropped mop, remembering how, when I'd cried on her shoulder, I'd smelt leather. Thoughtfully, I look down at my leather jacket and wonder.

I reach the door and hesitate, knowing in my heart what I will find, but still hardly able to believe it. Taking a deep breath, I push the door wide open and enter to find – nothing. No body, no bloodstains, no trace of habitation at all; the room mocks me with its emptiness.

Suddenly exhausted from the strangeness of it all, I wearily go back downstairs and leave the house for the last time; pulling the front door shut behind me, I sink down on the step to consider things, feeling strangely at peace for the first time in years.

It's as if the events of the past hour have somehow cleansed me, leaving me drained but healed. I have finally been forced to face up to my nightmare and have survived it. I look at the phone in my hand, wondering how it's possible a call for help now, could have been answered twenty years ago, or was it the other way around? I shake my head in confusion, knowing I'd probably never work it all out. Slowly, I dial another number.

'Hello, Greg? It's Cass. Something's happened, and I really need to talk to you. Yes, that's right, talk. Please, Greg, it's important. There's things about me I feel you should know, stuff that...happened...to me, when I was a child. Could you meet me? Yes, at the flat? Ok, one hour then...oh, and Greg...I think I love you.'

The End...

Domestic Bliss

There's a domestic at number 21.
This is a quiet street, a nice street,
Implacable in its middle-class restraint,
Until the raised voices, the slamming doors,
The language, become too much,
Even for its normally apathetic residents,
And the lights go on, up and down the street.

There's a domestic at number 21.
Roused from sleep, windows are raised,
And women peer, clutching nighties to chests.
Their husbands going one step further,
Letting down their individual drawbridges,
They lurk, in uncertain belligerence, on doorsteps,
And comments are exchanged, up and down the street.

There's a domestic at number 21.
Like a pebble thrown into a pond, its ripples spread,
As, for the briefest of moments,
The street is shaken from its normal façade,
Its everyday sameness, to bond
In mutual, nightwear-clad, outrage,
And residential unrest, up and down the street.

There was a domestic at number 21.
When the police finally arrived,
As usual, twenty-three minutes too late,
All had settled into an uneasy peace.
Slowly, reluctantly, people retreated indoors,
The moment over, nothing more to see,
And the kettles went on, up and down the street.

Don't Hurt Me

So, this is love.

Stretching blissfully in his arms, she thought of their first meeting, of him standing at her till with an armful of books. She'd served him, heart thumping beneath her prim cardigan, never imagining he'd...

'I don't want to hurt you,' he murmured, stroking her face.

She blushed at the intensity of his look.

As if he ever could.

Days later, headlines screamed of the dismembered woman's body, mutilated, defiled beyond belief.

He read them, mouth twisting in irony.

'I only said I didn't want to hurt you, not that I wouldn't.'

What are the Chances?

Of all the people in the world, meeting the one destined to be your soulmate...come on, what are the chances?

What are the Chances?

It was Max who first saw her. They were ambling home, worn out from the walk, when he abruptly parked his ample backside on the pavement and looked up at Adam, wrinkling his brows and slitting his eyes, in the way Adam found endearing, but girlfriends past had thought creepy – 'He's doing it again!' 'Adam, make your dog stop looking at me like that.'

Now, he uttered a breathy, chesty, growl, stared across the street. So, Adam looked too, and saw her.

Oh wow, his befuddled brain managed. Drop. Dead. Gorgeous! Long, glossy, shampoo ad, hair, a glimmering curtain of caramel, toffee and coffee, it rippled over her shoulders, simply begging to be touched. And then there was the body. Oh, the body, the body!

Not too tall, not too short. Not fat, not by any stretch of the imagination, but not too scrawny either. No, she was toned. That was the word, he decided, definitely toned. He'd be willing to bet long hours had been spent with a personal trainer to achieve that look.

The top was loose, filmy, feminine, expensive looking; the skirt figure hugging, ending at the knee, it showcased amazing legs, which seemed to stretch on forever, all the way down to slim feet clad in killer heels.

Gazing into the jewelers' shop window, she was oblivious to his scrutiny. Probably just as well, Adam thought wryly, watching appreciatively, as she shifted position on those heels – how did she manage to stay upright on them – thrusting her hips forward, spine arching provocatively.

'So out of your league, mate,' he muttered under his breath. Max whined, patting at his knee with a large paw, reminding him of more important things, namely, home, water and dinner, in that order.

'I know, I know,' Adam murmured, scratching Max behind the ear, but still he lingered, something about the woman, her perfection, her poise, her total absorption in the contents of the shop window, drawing his attention. As he watched, she rested her long, perfectly manicured, talons briefly on the glass of the window. It was plain by those nails, she'd never done an honest day's work in her life, and Adam ruefully thrust his own hands into his pockets, hands which built, toiled and laboured.

No, he decided, it was obvious this vision was a five-star restaurant type of girl, whereas he – Adam shook his head in resignation, he was more a beer and pizza in front of the TV type of guy. Resigned to waiting, Max scratched, long and hard, and Adam glared at him. 'Don't tell me you've got fleas again,' he groaned.

Max managed to look defiant, offended and sheepish, all at the same time. Adam bit back a laugh, wondering how Miss Perfect across the way would react to his flea-bitten hound.

'Probably leave town in the first limo,' he muttered. 'Oh well, love me, love my dog.' He shook Max's lead. 'Come on, you, home.'

Max got up, trotting happily by his side, eager now the scent of home and food was in his nose. Adam couldn't help casting a last, lingering, glance at her, hoping for just one sign she was human. It could be anything, a scratch, a sigh, a sneeze, anything to break the perfection, anything to give him the courage to maybe cross the street, maybe talk to her...

'Who are you trying to kid, mate,' he thought in sour amusement. 'You? Approach some strange woman in the street and chat her up? Oh yeah, what are the chances of that?'

This is ridiculous, Alex thought. She had to move, she had to get home. She couldn't stand here, glued to the pavement, staring intently into some dumb, overpriced, jewelers shop forever.

'You can do it, girl,' she muttered. Gingerly, carefully, shifted her feet in those stupid, stupid shoes, bracing her aching spine, wincing as ten screaming blisters located where her toes used to be, registered their disapproval at the move.

'Damn you, Mother,' she swore under her breath. It was all her mother's fault, she decided fiercely. Definitely, mum's fault she was now stuck, halfway home, because she literally. Could. Not. Take. Another. Step. In these ridiculous shoes that mum had insisted, no, let's get the facts straight, had forced her to wear.

It was all because she and mum shared the same birthday. It had always caused problems. Her whole life, Alex had been torn, between pleasing her mother on their special day, and pleasing herself.

Some years back, a compromise had been reached, the day belonged to mum, well, up until after lunch anyway. The rest of the day, and, more importantly, the evening, belonged to Alex.

This year, the day started out alright, even kind of fun, with a girly champagne breakfast at mum's, but had quickly deteriorated with a visit to the beauty parlour. Alex should have been prepared, after all, mum had dropped some fairly mammoth hints, but, she could never have anticipated the lengths to which her mother would go, all to achieve a perfect plastic daughter, ready to pose with mum for a portrait photo to take pride of place over her parents' fireplace.

All morning, Alex had been waxed, preened, plucked and polished. Terrifying false nails had been stuck onto her unwilling fingers – 'Really, Alex, just because you make your living gardening, doesn't mean you need to have half a ton of dirt under your nails.'

Her hair had been blow dried and scorched into submission, its normal riotous mass of curls tamed and flattened, and Alex shuddered at the amount of product it had taken, before her hair had finally surrendered.

Then, from a bag whose designer logo was enough to almost bring Alex out in hives, mum had produced the clothes. The skirt, its clinging shortness making Alex, more accustomed to mud spattered jeans, squirm uncomfortably; the blouse, which she actually didn't mind, and the shoes. No, not shoes, she corrected herself, manmade instruments of torture.

But, she'd suffered, because it was for mum, and, at the end of the day, most of the time, mum was brilliant. She hid well her disappointment she was not Alexandra, the perfect daughter she'd ordered. Accepted that, somehow, there'd been a mix up in the gene pool, which meant instead she'd ended up with the outdoorsy, tomboy, rough-and-ready, never-wear-a-skirt-if-she-could-possibly-help-it, landscape gardener daughter, Alex.

Aside from the odd pained look or heavy sigh, when Alex arrived in her disreputable old truck, sending the neighbourhood into a fit of tutting; or when Bella jumped up with muddy paws at one of her new designer outfits, mum never ever said a word.

At the thought of Bella, Alex stifled a groan. That settled it. She had to get home somehow. Bella had been shut in since this morning and, although good at crossing her legs, she'd be hungry for her dinner now. From past experience, Alex also knew she was likely to pee on the kitchen floor, simply as a way of expressing her disapproval at being left so long.

Which further reminded her, tomorrow she needed to pay a visit to the pet shop and pick up some more flea powder. Last night, watching a film, Bella's not inconsiderable weight sprawled over her on the sofa, lazily licking remains of a pizza from the box, Alex was pretty sure, something had jumped...

But, that was tomorrow, now she had to get home and change for the surprise birthday party she knew her friends had arranged for her. At least, it was supposed to be a surprise, but, Mel was incapable of telling a convincing lie. So, when Alex spotted her in the supermarket last week, buying enough booze to sink a battleship, Mel's blushes and stuttered explanation of 'stocking up for Christmas' – really, in May? – had put a smile on Alex's lips and a spring in her step.

But first, she had to get home. Experimentally, she wiggled her feet in the shoes. Pain exploded. How did women wear these wretched things, day in, day out? She glanced at the nails, well, one small mercy, at least her hair, nails and make up already looked amazing for tonight. She couldn't wait to see her friends' faces when they got a load of her new, temporary, look, because it was only temporary. Alex knew the hair wouldn't last beyond the next shower. As for the nails, well, she was constructing Mrs Watson's Italian rockery garden tomorrow, she doubted they would survive intact through that.

Nothing for it, stifling a curse, Alex snatched off the shoes, placed her burning feet flat on the welcome coolness of the pavement, groaning with relief. She'd walk home barefooted, she'd done it before, it wasn't far and anything was better than wearing them a moment longer.

She turned to go and saw them. She noticed the dog first, plodding away, obviously exhausted from a good, long, walk, saggy backend swaying, reminding her so much of Bella, she smiled. The guy pacing beside the dog also looked tired, his shoulders hunched dejectedly. Must have been some walk, she reflected, then dismissed them, her mind already on the forthcoming party.

She wondered whether Simon would be there. One of her oldest friends, Simon had been away on business for several weeks and she'd missed him. She remembered how, before he'd left, she and the gang had been invited round to dinner. Partly to say farewell, partly to christen his new dining room. Duly, they'd all admired the beauty of the new extension, Simon singing the praises of the local builder he'd discovered.

'He's simply brilliant,' he'd enthused. 'Nothing was too much trouble, he's a great bloke and so professional, came when he said he would and the job cost almost exactly what he estimated.'

There was a pause, while they'd all agreed how unusual

that was; then, Simon's eyes had narrowed thoughtfully at Alex. Pouring her more wine, he'd leant closer, a grin of amusement creasing the corners of his eyes.

'You know, he'd be absolutely perfect for you, Alex. A completely practical, outdoorsy, kind of guy, he even owns a mangy mutt he's every bit as obsessed about, as you are about Bella.' Although Alex had laughed with the rest of them, she'd felt the faintest twinge of interest, had even been slightly disappointed, when Simon went away without anything more being said.

But then, meeting your soul mate on a blind date?

'Really, Alex,' she muttered to herself, as she limped painfully down the road. 'What are the chances...?'

Trudging home, feeling strangely miserable and a bit out of sorts, Adam felt his phone vibrate in his pocket and fished it out. 'Hello?'

'Hi Adam, its Simon, Simon Baxter, listen, are you free tonight? Only, we're throwing a friend a surprise birthday party, and I was wondering...what are the chances you'd be able to come...?'

The End...

The Visit

Autumn visited my garden today.
With rustling steps, it crept,
Hesitated, unsure of its welcome,
Resting skeletal fingers on my shoulder.
I felt it, in the chill of a cloud banished sun.
Tasted it, in the rawness of the breeze.
Heard it, in the loose rattling of leaves,
And year lost memories flickered,
Russet red and conker brown.

In a sky suddenly dulled with middle age,
An arrowhead formation of geese flew,
Instinct pulling their heavy, grey bodies,
Ever southward, strong wings carrying them,
Away, away, honking their farewells,
Until I was left, alone, in the silent garden.
The sun surged from its downy prison, and,
Reluctantly, autumn stepped back, whispering,
Not yet, not quite yet, but soon ... soon ...

Lifework

I hate housework, it is my bane,
My nemesis, the constant nag at my ear,
And yet, as I've come to realise,
It's also a metaphor for my life.
In that, most of the time, I cruise,
Jogging steadily through my days,
A wipe down here, a spit and a polish there,
Doing just enough to get by,
To remain on the right side of social acceptance,
Caught in the endless routine, round and round,
My weeks and minutes spin, unload and reload,
Use it and wash it, then use it again.

Employing tactics of fire-fighting and tunnel vision,
Picking up as I go, I tell myself it's enough,
Whilst, all around me, the dust settles,
Gently, persistently, it pervades and invades,
The debris of a life in crisis, a clogging reminder,
Of things I should have done, should have remembered,
Visits I should have made, forms I should have returned,
Vouchers I should have used, friends I should have called.
And, in the darkest, most secret, corners of my life,
The places I try never to examine too closely,
The cobwebs twist and thicken, grimy and black,
Obscuring what lies beneath, strangling the truth.

Then comes a day of sudden invigoration,
Windows and doors are thrown violently open,
And fresh air gusts through the rooms of my life.
Cupboards and corners are emptied,
Contents examined, scrubbed and sorted.
Ditch the useless, the defunct, and the broken.
Get rid of, clean up and start again.
In the self-satisfied glow of the newly converted,
Resolutions and promises are made, to stay on top,
To control my life, not let it control me, yet, all around,
On the shiny surfaces of my freshly laundered existence,
The dust once again, quietly, persistently, begins to settle.

Family

Matters

He's looked for her for so many years, but, when Albert finally finds his granddaughter, she's not what he expected.

Family Matters

The first thing he notices about her, is the stud through her nose. It both fascinates and annoys him. He stares at its blunt ugliness, which detracts from, and yet, strangely, draws attention, to her pert, freckled, nose. She is pretty, he supposes, in a modern, sort of way.

Her features seem to him sharp and angular, and he finds himself remembering another face from long ago. A face once so dear to him, but now, through the kind amnesia of time, remembered indistinctly. Surely, no woman's face could have been so perfect, so flawless.

He clears his throat and the girl looks up, mobile phone clutched tightly in her right hand. He wonders at the total dependence of today's youth upon such a brash, intrusive, gadget, then smiles slightly at himself, for such old man notions.

He clears his throat again, unsure what to say, how to begin. She lifts her brow in questioning silence. There, that movement, that expression, a fleeting snapshot of familiarity that leaves him with no more doubts. She is the one.

'Jennifer?' Even the name is right, an anglicised version of that long-ago name, sighed in love and guilty abandonment during sweet, stolen, moments.

'Yeah?' The short answer snaps him back to the present.

'Do you know who I am?' he asks. 'My name is Albert

and I am your grandfather. I have been looking for you all your life.'

She shrugs. 'Well, here I am'. Her answer is surly, almost to the point of rudeness. For a moment, he is tempted to simply turn and walk away. Go back to his nice, orderly life, with his little pre-set routines and habits.

Then, he sees the hand clutching that wretched mobile phone is not a steady one. It trembles. In a flash, he sees the nervousness and uncertainty, buried beneath the cocky bravado.

'How much do you know about your family? What did your mother tell you, before she died?' He keeps his voice low and steady, the way you would talk to a frightened animal.

She shrugs again. 'I know my grandmother was French, and got herself knocked up by some British guy. I know my mother also married a British man and moved back here, they had me, then managed to get themselves killed in a car crash, leaving me on my own. That about cover it?'

He considers her words, the bravado behind them, then feels the first drop of rain on his cheek. Turning, he motions to the chauffeur, who brings a large umbrella from the car. Unfurling it, hands it to Albert, who sits beside Jennifer on the park bench, the umbrella covering them both.

She starts at this subtle display of power, asks, with almost childlike awe, 'Are you very rich?'

Albert smiles, remembering the long, hard, road to achieve all he has, and how he would have given it all up, just to have what most men take for granted, the right to live his life with the woman he loved and his child.

'Will you tell me, tell me about her and about you. Why you left her, what happened?'

Albert looks for the first time into Jennifer's eyes, realises they are familiar, not the colour, this girl's eyes are an intense blue, whereas Genevieve's were the deepest, softest, brown imaginable, but, the deep, almond, shape of them, with that slight upward tilt and those thick, dark lashes.

He takes a deep breath, to steady himself, and tells here. Tells of himself and her grandmother, both impossibly young, meeting in war-torn, fifties, France, of them falling instantly and irrevocably in love.

He tells of their brief, too brief, time together, how he is forced to leave her to return home to his ailing father, promising to return for her as soon as he could, making her promise to wait for him. He tells how, on coming home, he found a father so ill, he could not think of returning to Genevieve as quickly as planned. How, when his father finally died, he then had to cope with unexpectedly having responsibilities thrust upon his young shoulders, the family firm, his mother's inability to function alone.

Then, months later than planned, than promised, his

return to France to claim his bride, only to find her gone, the whole family gone, and the villagers hostile and suspicious, refusing to give him any information at all. He tells of desperately, frantically, searching for her, and of the slowly dawning realisation of the impossibility of the task.

'So,' says Jennifer. 'You gave up!'

'Oh no,' he responds softly. 'I never stopped looking. I had to come home eventually to run the firm, look after my mother, but, every occasion I could, I went back to France, searched everywhere, tried everything to find them. It was no use. It was as if the Dupont family had vanished into thin air.'

He speaks of long, lonely, years, constantly hoping and searching, until, eventually, he was wealthy enough to pay others, more experienced than him, to continue the search. He tells of that day, still etched in his heart, when he was given two pieces of paper.

One, showing Genevieve had given him a child, born almost exactly nine months after their final day together, when youth, and the despair of lovers about to be parted, had combined to make what happened between them inevitable.

How he had wept, as he had looked at the second piece of paper, which informed him she had paid the ultimate price for their love, had died, whilst struggling to bring their daughter into the world, a daughter she had lived long enough to call Alberta.

Albert paused, took a handkerchief from his pocket, wiped away the tears that flowed freely, as he remembered how a piece of him had died that day. Suddenly, a small hand is hesitantly placed over his, and he looks up into blue eyes, in which he can see his own sadness reflected.

'I didn't know,' she shakes her head. 'I didn't know any of this.'

'How could you have,' he replies. 'It was my fault, if I had known, had thought about what might have happened, I would have brought her back with me, I would never have left her, maybe, who knows, maybe if she'd had the baby in a British hospital, rather than in some backwater hovel, she wouldn't have died.'

'So, did you then move on with your life?' asks Jennifer. 'Now that you knew she was dead, did you then marry someone else, have children?'

He shakes his head, shocked. 'No, how could I have? Genevieve was the one person in the world for me, there could be no other, and, besides, I had to continue the search, I had to find my daughter, your mother.'

'But, you didn't find her,' states Jennifer.

'Not until years later, when it was too late, she and your father had been killed in a car crash, and you had vanished into the system somewhere. It was not until a couple of months ago, all the loose ends came together, and I finally tracked you down to your place of work, well, one of your places of work. By the time I got there, you'd already moved on to another job,'

He coughed in dry amusement. 'You appear to have had a rather varied career.'

Jennifer shrugs. 'Yeah, I never do seem to stick around long enough to collect my P45.'

'What are you doing now?'

'Waitressing.'

'Oh, are you a good waitress then?'

'No' Jennifer grins, 'I'm a completely rubbish one, that's why I can never keep a job for very long.'

'Please,' Albert pauses, unsure how to say what he so desperately wants to ask of her. 'Come home with me, Jennifer.'

She looks at him, her gaze level and reflective. 'You know,' she says, 'When I got your letter, telling me you were my grandfather, and that you wanted to meet me, I thought well, go and see him, but, really, what's the point. There's nothing he can give you, it's all too little, too late, but now...I don't know, learning the truth, well, you're the only family I have, and that's gotta mean something, hasn't it?'

Albert nods his head slowly. 'Yes, my dear, it means everything. So, will you come?' He can feel the almost pleading note in his voice, hopes she cannot hear his desperation.

'Ok,' she says. 'I guess, we can give it a go, and see what

happens'.

Albert beams at her, and she sees a glimpse of the handsome, young, man her grandmother fell in love with.

Chivalrously, he holds out his arm to her. Jennifer hesitates, feeling the heavy importance of the moment, until, with almost debutante shyness, she places her arm on his. Walks with him, to where the car is waiting patiently for them by the park gates.

He seems a nice old boy, she thinks, obviously desperate to make things up to her. She'd heard someone had been looking for her. So many cards he'd handed out to people who knew her, she'd been told, warned. She'd googled him. Wondering what a millionaire could possibly want with the likes of her, did a little research of her own. The truth wasn't hard to find.

So, it might be more advantageous to stick around, see how the land lay, get herself written into the will, rather than just take whatever she can get and run. Yes, that might be a better plan...

The End...

Relative Endings

As deaths go, it wasn't a bad one. Slipping peacefully into much needed sleep; surrounded by his loved ones. Being dimly aware of a sudden jolt to his body; then, nothing...

An ambulance came, but was too late.

The youngest paramedic, as green as his uniform, surveyed the scene with still shockable eyes.

'What do you think happened?'

His older colleague, more seasoned to their job's macabre whims, shrugged.

'Damn fool, probably fell asleep at the wheel and lost control.'

He looked at the row of body bags on the verge and sighed.

'Shame the rest of his family were in the car with him.'

The Child and the Mouse

There's something horrid on the lawn.
Something nasty. Something dead.
Fascinated, the child squats,
Feeling the nip of wellies against bare legs,
And stares, and stares.
An eye, bead black and empty, stares back.
Silky whiskers tremble in the breeze,
Over lips drawn back forever in a deathly grimace,
Showing small, flint like teeth, sharp and yellow.
Tiny fingers on tiny paws, folded neatly,
Delicately, as though at prayer.
Soft brown fur, which calls to be touched.
To be stroked, ever so gently, with a finger.
Yet, the child's hands remain clenched.

A stick is fetched to poke and probe,
Moving aside long grass to reveal awfulness,
Gaping nothing where the rest should be.
Disney charm waist up; Stephen King waist down.
The child prods, and pink coils slither and glisten,
A horror story, as things ripple, squelch,
A fly buzzes, disturbed, it angrily drones its displeasure.
The child's mother is fetched, and the child watches,
Respectfully silent, as the thing that once lived,
Is wrapped in newspaper and disposed of in the bin.
Boiling water poured over rusty, red grass,
Until no trace is left, and play can resume.

Later, in that dusky land between awake and asleep,
The child remembers...
Tiny folded hands, a bead black eye
Gazing blindly at the print of a newspaper shroud.
And the child is sad.

A Strange
Kind of Love

Matt had always known his girlfriend Leeza was strange, but was he prepared for just how strange she really was?

A Strange Kind of Love

If it hadn't been for the long overdue argument with my boss, which ended with me quitting and walking out; I would have got home too late, and everything would have been different.

Losing my job didn't bother me in the slightest, I'm one of the best IT consultants in London, possibly even in England. Hell, let's not be modest here, when it comes to computers, there ain't nothing I don't know, or can't do with them. I knew my worth, knew I could pick up another job easily, maybe, finally make the decision to go freelance.

So, that's why I was walking home on a Saturday morning when, by rights, I should still have been at work. The relief of finally being free of that place was quite intoxicating, and put a real spring in my step, especially as I was going home to Leeza.

Leeza, my amazing, crazy, eccentric, girlfriend. She's my reason for existing, the most fantastic, unpredictable, wildest, thing. to ever happen to me. I can't believe it's been less than a year since we met.

We've only been an item for six months, and I only managed to persuade her to move in with me four weeks ago. Already, I couldn't imagine her not being there when I got home, pottering around the tiny scrap of a garden, or in the kitchen, concocting one of her bizarre, but delicious, vegetarian meals.

I absolutely adore her, despite, or maybe because of,

her strangeness, that otherworldly manner of hers. She has this wonderful knack, of making someone feel they are the most interesting person in the world, and it's not an act, people genuinely fascinate her. 'Everyone has a story to tell, Matt,' she once told me. 'Everyone has information to share and can be learnt from.'

Maybe, it's because she's a researcher, that she's so interested in everything. Don't ask me what kind of researching she does, or even whom she works for, because I don't know. I did once really press her to tell me, early on in our relationship, but, she became so evasive and upset, that I never questioned her about it again.

I got the feeling it was some kind of secret, maybe she worked for one of the government agencies. Anyway, it didn't matter; the fact is I'm completely crazy over her. She could tell me she's a trained assassin, I wouldn't care.

Even the way we met was a bit strange. One evening, she was just there, in the pub, where I and my other computer nerd friends meet. I noticed her straightaway, who wouldn't notice Leeza? There's something about her, I can't put my finger on it, she's just...different.

Anyway, like I said, I noticed her, couldn't stop looking at her all evening. Left to my own devices, that's probably where it would have ended, and I'm still not really too sure how it all happened.

One moment, I was returning from the bar with my drink, the next I'd barged straight into her, spilling almost a whole pint down the front of her dress. As an icebreaker with a beautiful woman, I wouldn't normally recommend it, but, it certainly worked that night.

By the time I'd spluttered out apologies, dabbed inefficiently at her with a tissue, borrowed a damp cloth from an amused and sympathetic barmaid, apologised about another zillion times, bought drinks to replace the spilt ones, ushered her over to my friends, and made introductions all round, we were friends.

After that, it seemed natural, whenever we were in the pub, Leeza would appear. I do remember one strange thing that happened. It was a few weeks later, we were standing at the bar, when I turned to her and said 'By the way, Leeza who? What is your surname?'

For a second, there was a panic stricken look on her face, as she stared at the bottles behind the bar, almost as if seeking inspiration. 'Gordon,' she said, fixing me with one of her wide-eyed, gamine, smiles. 'That's my name, Leeza Gordon.'

Leeza is strange sometimes. What am I saying? Leeza is strange most of the time.

Then there's the fact, she's a complete and utter technophobe. She doesn't seem to know or understand anything about technology. When Leeza discovered what I did for a living, she would question me endlessly about it and hang upon my every word, even making notes.

When I teased her about it, she explained work were

installing new computers, and she didn't want to look too dumb when it came to using them.

I offered to teach her on my home computers, she accepted, and that's how our relationship began. She simply blew me away with her fresh originality, her quirky, different, perspective on life, and the way she gave love with an almost childlike, wholehearted, gusto, seeming to want to live every day as if it were her last. Most of all, she made me believe in myself, like there was nothing we couldn't achieve together.

Yes, as I walked home on that warm, spring, morning, I felt pretty good. Life was sweet, I'd left a job I hated, and I was in love with the most amazing woman in the world.

'Hey Leeza, guess why I'm home so early,' I called out, as I let myself in, headed for the bedroom, where I could see movement. 'I've finally done it, I've left...' the words died on my lips as I walked into the room, saw what she was doing. She was packing, judging by the look of stunned guilt on her face, it wasn't for a surprise holiday for us!

'What are you doing?' I demanded. 'Leeza, what the hell's going on? Are you leaving me?'

'Matt, you're home early,' It was the way she couldn't look me in the eye, that upset me the most.

'Oh, I'm so sorry!' I exclaimed angrily. 'Spoilt your plans, did I? How was it supposed to happen then, Leeza? Was I gonna get home and find you gone? For god's sake, Leeza, why? Just tell me why? I thought we were happy!'

To my horror I heard my voice break.

'We were. We are.' Leeza didn't even try to hold back her tears. 'Matt, I can't explain. I'm not leaving you, but I have to go. I'm so sorry; it's all my fault. I knew this would happen one day. I should never have got involved with you, but I fell in love. I wasn't supposed to, it wasn't part of the plan, and now I have to go.'

She turned to stuff some more things into her bag, and I could have sworn I heard her mutter, 'I have my orders.'

I can't explain why I said what I said next. It must have been in my subconscious all along, an answer, to all the strange and unexplainable things that Leeza did and was.

'Is it because you're from another world?'

Leeza span round, eyes wide with shock. 'How did you...? What...that's...don't be ridiculous, Matt!'

But, it was too late, I'd seen the truth in her eyes, and it made sense of everything. I could almost hear all the pieces of the puzzle falling into place, click, click, click.

'So that's it,' I breathed. 'I knew it! Are you an exiled princess from a strange, alternate, reality?'

Leeza sighed in amused exasperation. 'Oh Matt!' she said. 'You've been reading far too many fantasy stories. My world is not an alternative reality; it's simply parallel to this one. Sometimes, portals open briefly between our worlds, and it's possible to pass through. A princess? I'm not a princess, I told you what I am, I'm a researcher. That's why I was sent here, to London, to try and learn as much about computers as I could. We don't have them in my world, you see.'

My heart stood still. 'I see,' I said slowly, my mind racing frantically, putting two and two together. 'So, that's why you're with me, for my computer knowledge.'

'No, Matt, oh no! I know how it must look, but it's not like that at all. Initially, yes, that's why I arranged to meet you. But, that's not why I fell in love with you, why I moved in with you.'

'So why did you then?' I demanded. 'Knowing you'd be going back, why did you move in?'

'The portals between our worlds are very unpredictable. Nobody knows when or where one will occur, until they do, then they're only open for a matter of hours. One has opened today, here, in London, and I've got to go home. I'm so sorry, Matt, I kept hoping I'd have more time with you.'

I stared at her, unable to believe I was going to lose her, so soon after finding her. 'Take me with you!' I suddenly blurted. 'Please Leeza, I mean it. Wouldn't it be better, for me to teach your world about computers, rather than you try and remember what I've told you, and get it all wrong. Is it possible? Can I come with you?'

A gleam of hope came into her eyes. 'Yes,' she said slowly. 'It is possible, it's been done before. But, oh Matt, are you sure? My world, it's very different from yours. There are very few people in my world compared to yours.

Women can only conceive just once in their lives, and then it must be with their lifemate, the one person who truly loves them. Both partners must be fully committed to creating and raising offspring. There are no unwanted children in my world, Matt. Every child is considered a precious gift.'

'It sounds like paradise,' I replied, thinking back to my own grim childhood, spent in a succession of children's homes, from which only hard work, and my innate computer skills had saved me.

'Leeza, nothing you can say would put me off. There's nothing left here for me if you go. Please, let me come.'

Tears sprang to her eyes again. 'Oh Matt,' she whispered, 'I was so desperate at leaving you. Yes, come, if you are sure it's what you truly want.'

I crossed the room in one bound and held her tightly. 'You try and stop me. Is there enough room for me to throw a few clothes in your bag?'

Leeza laughed and nodded, then her face grew serious again, and she pulled away from me. 'There's one other thing, Matt. I had to change my appearance to come here. This is not what I normally look like.'

I swallowed, visions of eight tentacled, slithery, things dancing in my head. 'Erm, right, what do you look like then? Can you show me?'

Leeza hesitated, then nodded, and put her hands to her ears. I'm not sure how she did it, but it was as if she pulled off her human ears to reveal sweet, little pointed ones underneath.

'Wow!' I gasped, hesitantly lifted a finger to touch them. To my delight, they were covered with fine, silky soft, silvery hairs.

'Wait,' she said, 'there's more,' and she put her hands to her eyes. Have you ever seen someone remove contacts? Well, that's exactly what Leeza did, only the eyes underneath were like no human eyes possible.

Imagine eyes with no whites or pupils, eyes the softest, clearest, sea green, imaginable. Leeza stood, watching me, as I gaped, open mouthed, in shock.

'Matt?' The question was in her voice, together with her fear of rejection.

'You're so beautiful!' I breathed. 'Like an elf or a pixie.' I started, as a sudden thought dawned. 'Is that why...?'

'Yes.' Leeza interrupted. 'The portals have been occurring since the dawn of time. We think, it must explain the abundance of references in your folklore and myths to fairy folk and other worlds.'

My head was spinning, then I noticed Leeza glance at the clock and frown. 'How much longer do we have?' I asked in concern.

'The portal will close in one hour. If you're coming with me, Matt, we must leave now.'

'Ok.' My decision had already been made. 'Put your eyes and ears back on, woman, and let's go!'

So, that's how I found myself hurrying, hand in hand with Leeza, down the streets of London, carrying the bag, so Leeza could consult with what she called the 'tracker'.

'Portals give out a certain type of energy only found in my world,' she explained. 'The tracker simply homes in on it. Ah, here we go!'

She led me into one of those short, industrial, lanes that dead-end at the Thames. About halfway down, on the right-hand side, there was a patch of what can only be described as otherness. You could only see it if you knew where to look.

Leeza stopped in front of it, turned to face me. 'Last chance to change your mind,' she said quietly.

I looked around me. At the end of the lane, I could see the bustle and noise of London. I took a deep breath, tightened my grip on her hand.

'Let's do it!'

Leeza smiled, took my hand and stepped backwards into the portal, pulled me through after. Like I said, sometimes, Leeza is strange.

The End

The Time Traveller

At the commencement of her journey,
She was an innocent,
Naïve of the hardships she faced.
Gradually, she learnt, time travelling to the future,
Was actually development of self.
Of time spent, learning, growing, changing.

On route, she created ambassadors of her DNA,
Sent them forward to a world,
More distant than she could ever imagine.
Still she travelled, gaining knowledge and experience
With each, quickly passing, decade.

Eventually, she reached her destination.
It had been a long, hard, voyage, yet, looking back,
It seemed the years had flown past, merging seamlessly,
Until she reached this point in time,
Ninety years in her future.
Journeys end.

Unicorn Dreams

**A fairy tale in rhyme for the young
and young at heart**

Unicorn Dreams

The baby unicorn was bored. The baby unicorn was lonely.
Here, in her shining land, so warm and safe and homely.
She shook free her mane, her thoughts all out of rhyme,
And her mother whispered low, Little One, it's time!

It's time for you to make a trip all unicorns make but twice.
Time for you to leave our land, so good and pure and nice.
For once we dwelt far away and lived as one with man,
And in their dreams, we walked. Little One, yes you can.

For men this is a special night, a blessed sacred eve,
For on this most magical night, many do believe,
A child was born to save them all, and for their sins atone.
And in their dreams, this holy night, you must go alone.

And on the shore of the shimmering Ocean of Dreams.
Dividing world from world, at least that's how it seems.
Her mother shook her horn in a sparkling blast of gold,
And a rainbow boat appeared with crimson sails unfurled.

Little One kissed her mother, and jumped aboard the boat,
And over waves of deepest dreams, the little craft did float.
Her heart beat fast and strong, at adventures yet to come,
At last the boat was still, and the Little One trotted on.

Into the dreams of a powerful king as he lay in his bed.
Yet all was dark and dreary, a dungeon in his head.
For all his power and might, family had he none.
She shook her mane in pity, and the Little One trotted on.

A serving lad came next, truly the lowest of them all,
Yet all was colourful in his dreams, a feast, a party, a ball!
He danced with a pretty wife and friends, all having fun.
She stamped with pleasure, and the Little One trotted on.

A princess lay in a silken bed, her dreams a sea of tears.
Forced to marry an unknown king, her head full of fears.
As she sighed, wished for love, but cried all hope was gone.

She bent her head in sadness, and Little One trotted on.

To a humble little kitchen maid, so ragged, low and poor,
Memory of her wedding day made her happy heart soar.
Her groom was poor, it's true, but knew he was the one.
She tossed her horn with joy, and the Little One trotted on.

A pirate slept on his ship, dreaming of gold and its glitter.
With no joy in his cold, hard heart, its value was as litter.
He tossed and turned in anguish at evil deeds he'd done.
She neighed low with terror, and the Little One trotted on.

An old, simple parson, dreams full of thoughts of others.
Of a lifetime of giving, to all those sisters and brothers.
Fretting for ways to help, his heart so good and strong.
She wiped away her tears, and the Little One trotted on.

At dawn she sailed again, across the Ocean of Dreams.
Thinking of all she'd learnt, how life is not what it seems.
When mother came to greet her, her kisses warm and true.
Little One said, Oh, dear mother! Things I must tell to you.

I've seen a crown and power, do not happiness bring.
I've seen the lowest born, can have good reason to sing.
I've found freedom to choose, is worth its weight in gold.
And rags can't humble you, when it's true love you hold.

I've learnt a life is empty, when lived only for the sword.
But a generous and a giving life, can be its own reward.
Her mother touched her horn. You've learnt well, she said,
Men's hearts are so revealed, when sleeping in their bed.

Another year passed swiftly in shimmering unicorn land,
And Mother said. It is time to go, for you to understand.
The power of a unicorn, as it travels through the night.
The glory of its passing, can turn wrong to right.

So again, the Little One went, in her boat with sail of red,
And all wondrous things she saw, as they lay in their bed.
Could this be that lonely king, with a daughter on his knee,
And a beautiful queen by his side, how did this come to be?

That scared, unhappy princess who came to be his bride.
Looked deep into her husband's heart, saw the hope inside.
True love grew in an instant, to last their whole sweet life,
And gladly did the princess marry, happy to be his wife.

Their daughter's rosy nurse? With her loving, kindly heart,
Loves her royal charge, but from her husband did not part.
The happy king employed him, a royal gardener now, is he.
Growing flowers of such beauty, for all the world to see.

What of that evil pirate, with heart so twisted and black?
He met the faithful parson, as he led his men in an attack.
That good old man spoke softly, words of hope and trust,
The pirate did repent, vowing to change his life, he must.

So together with the parson, he roamed the ocean blue.
Giving away all his gold, looking for good deeds to do.
She saw peace in his heart, his spirit so pure and strong.
Neighed aloud with glory, and the Little One trotted on.

Christmas bells are chiming, as she is homeward bound,
Little One sighs with pleasure, at the goodwill she's found.
And as sleepers awaken, to a bright and Christmas Day,
Little One sails in her rainbow boat, singing all the way.

She returns home to her mother, glad her work is done.
Gazing at her shining land and singing her unicorn song
About her journey, in dreams where we love and weep.
Her mother softly kisses her, and the Little One fell asleep.

Lifesong

**If there is life on other worlds, what would it
be like? And what would they make of us?**

Chapter One. . .

It was a glorious night for his passing on. As the twin moons rose and darkness fell, she reflected how perfect it all was, how he would have loved the beauty of this night, would have appreciated the rightness of the traditional ritual, taken comfort from it. Except. He wasn't here. And it was left to her alone to take comfort where she could.

So many had gathered to send him on his way, many faces she knew, many unfamiliar. It did not surprise her. Her grandsire had been well known for the generosity of his heart and the wisdom of his words, dispensing one as freely as the other.

Taking a deep breath, she adjusted her cloak and stepped lightly onto the path. It must be begun. She must be the one to begin it. At her approach, the singing, which had been low, muted and harmonious, rose in unison, gloried and soared, as the singers skillfully twisted the strands of what had been his life, offered it to all as benediction.

Slowly, she paced until she reached the apex of the rise, saw the group of elders who awaited her, flaming torch in hand, their lifesong flowing from them in wise, measured notes, their faces dignified with the sagacity of their age.

She reached them, and bowed in acknowledgement of their status. Taking the torch from them, she felt its heat on her face, its sparks dazzling her eyes until the darkness beyond glittered in reflection. Leaving them, she crested the hill, saw the pyre waiting, her grandsire's body wrapped in its ceremonial robes.

Two council members stopped her, staffs crossed to bar her path, demanding to know her business. In accordance with custom she sang of her grandsire, of his life, his death, of her duty, as his much beloved grandchild, to send his lifesong on its final journey into the heavens to join the universal great song.

They bent their heads in recognition of her right, lowered their staffs until the points crossed on the ground before her. Carefully, holding the torch aloft, she stepped over them and walked to the pyre.

She waited, head bowed in acknowledgement of the solemnity of the moment, the perfection of the rites, until the funeral song had reached its pinnacle and it was time to play her part. Softly at first, then gaining in ascendancy, she wove her notes into the whole. Joyfully offering her thanks for his presence in her life, singing of the many kindnesses her grandsire had shown her, his talent for songsculpting, which he had passed on to her.

Briefly, she touched on superficial sorrow he was no longer there to guide her, then let her throat open in sublime knowledge of the new song he was now part of. That great, all-encompassing song, which weaved and twisted throughout existence, sweeping up all before it into one immense, perfect, never ending, constantly harmonious stream of sound.

Finally, moments or hours later, the singers stopped, the funeral song ended. The final flawless note echoed into ringing silence, and all joined for a moment in still contemplation.

Then, she stepped forward and thrust the burning brand deep into the heart of the pyre.

Much later, long after the ceremony had finally ended and all had departed, she was alone in their dwelling place. The liquid perfection of the dawn lulled her, and she sat on the step, the doors to the dwelling and her heart open to absorb the last drops of sunrise. She sang, softly and without purpose, a gently lilting melody. It touched on awareness her own lifesong must now be adjusted, that the hole created by her grandsire's passing needed to be smoothed over.

She understood that he was not really gone, that he had merely passed on to a new place, a better place, where life eternal flowed through the stars and planets. Yet...he had gone. He was not here with her. She was alone.

Crossly, she told herself this was not so. How could she be alone with so many others for companionship? When every day, if she chose, she could spend time with friends and neighbours. When her workshop always hummed with the busyness of those come to barter their goods for her much sought-after sculptures. No, she was not alone. Yet...she was lonely.

There was a disturbance in the undergrowth, a tiny squeak. With her heightened senses, she felt the demise of a small creature, the abrupt cessation of its lifesong. An instant later, Lani, her cat, stepped forward, a tiny creature dangling from her jaws.

Trotting past, Lani angled her head to look up, ears flattening, as if warning her to try and deny her this prize. She smiled at the cat's antics, feeling sorry for the rodent's demise, yet amused by the smugness of the cat's lifesong which settled into a happy, rumbling purr, as Lani crouched down and crunched on tiny bones.

Distracted, her own song ended, she tilted her head to survey the flaming sky, awed and humbled by its eternal majesty. Her grandsire had enjoyed contemplating the heavens, theorising on the life that possibly existed on those far away worlds. Often, discussion had led to gentle debate, as he placed before her new and alarming ideas. That the lifesong of their occupants might be very different to their own. Maybe, he'd even suggested, and she had shuddered with horror at the very thought, there was no lifesong on those glimmering distant specks of light.

Here, agreement had parted. She could not conceive of a world without lifesong, a world whose occupants existed in silence, bereft of the music which shaped reality. How could such beings survive without becoming insane? Even the simplest of animals recognised the natural harmony of life.

An ant, carrying a leaf back to his colony, danced to the music of his race, his lifesong busy and ordered. Birds, glorying in the freedom of the skies, their lifesong erupting in wildly spontaneous notes of purest sound, embodied the very essence of the great song which embraced and surrounded all.

From the humblest single celled being, she'd argued, to the more complex and emotive animals such as themselves, all paced their allotted lifespan to their own individual lifesong. To not sing, to not even be aware of the great song...such a thing was impossible.

Her grandsire had laughed at her discomfort, softly singing words of ease and reconciliation, until she had smiled again, dismissing his wild ideas as the stuff of childish nightmares. Impossible and inconceivable, and yet, she shifted uncomfortably on the hard, wooden step, remembering occasions when she had not been allowed to know his thoughts. Those times when the elders came, and they were closeted for long sessions within her grandsire's private chamber.

During these visits, she'd attempted to keep busy, to create, yet her song had been distracted, disjointed with bizarre impressions of what was occurring behind the firmly closed door. Knowing these frequent meetings with the elders to be a great honour for her grandsire, but still, resentful she was not included.

Afterwards, when the elders had taken their leave with

words and music of dignified thanks, he would look at her work. Brow creasing, tutting with displeasure at the awkward jaggedness of their outline, his eyes would rest thoughtfully on her, and she would know he was aware of her unease, perhaps even understood the source of those dark and unconnected thoughts which so distorted her sculptures.

And now he was gone. She was alone in the gathering bloom of the day, gazing at the heavens which had engendered such lively debate. Her loss at his passing swelled in her breast, and she gave words to her grief, gaining comfort at their shape and form, her song culminating in a long perfect note that soared ever upwards, reaching, straining, until suddenly she was amongst the stars looking down on the spinning beauty of her own planet.

Startled, frightened, heart pounding within her chest, she snapped back to reality, thrilling with the excited realisation she'd just travelled further than ever before, perhaps further than anyone had ever travelled before.

Eventually, words dwindled to a low, background hum, perfect pitch to the beating of her heart and the rushing of the blood in her veins. Drowsily, lids fell over eyes wearied from the ceremony of the night, the singing of her grandsire's lifesong, the acknowledgement of his existence, the flames of his funeral pyre still leapt in her memory, twisting and rising, a column of fire stretching to the sky, carrying his lifesong ever upwards.

Her thoughts slipped free from their mooring within her mind, roaming, seeking, questioning...

A place ... other ...

Heat ... intense and melting ...

Terror ... stark and immobilising ...

Its taste sickened in her mouth. The blaze roared like a wild beast, consuming what looked to be some sort of dwelling in front of her. It seemed, impossible as it was, she was actually inside another's thoughts and emotions. That she viewed through the eyes of another, eyes raw from smoke and the angry, frustrated tears of horrified shock.

She heard strange words issuing from her host's throat, words wrenched from a throat sand dry and hoarse from screaming. She felt the restraint of others. Knew the body she looked from to be held fast in the tight grip of two beings. Felt also the angry twisting as it fought to free itself; struggling to break away.

Further knew, should the being succeed, its aim was to plunge headlong into the inferno...

Her eyes opened. Once more brilliant sunlight dazzled overhead, her senses pulsed to the sounds of the morning, and she felt the steady pacing of her lifesong, her heart beating in tune to its rhythm.

Where had she been?

What had she been?

Still, behind her eyelids, she could see the bright hunger of the fire, feel the voraciousness of its appetite as it gobbled and consumed. Deep within, she could still emote to the wildly throbbing sting of bitter despair, experiencing again the overwhelming loss and pain of the strange being, whose mind and thoughts she had so briefly inhabited...

Chapter Two. . .

Distracted and anxious, she silently assembled a simple breakfast. Lacking appetite but aware that, after the ritualistic fasting in preparation for the funeral ceremony, sustenance of some description was required.

The food was a stabilising influence within her body. She sensed the nutrients being absorbed from the berries and nuts she had consumed, but tasted nothing in its consumption, her mind so shaped by the events of the night, and the strange vision she had been granted.

She slept fitfully. Again and again, her thoughts returning to the being she had briefly shared consciousness with, weeping silent tears of sympathy at his loss and anger. Wondering at her surety it had been male, but somehow knowing that raw, frustrated grief had been masculine in its intensity.

For many days after, her lifesong was disturbed, disordered, struggling with unquiet disharmony to attain that level of placid contentment she was accustomed to in her life and work.

Over and over, she would sternly instruct herself to desist in such thoughts. It had been a mere nightmare, a shade brought on by lack of food, the stresses of the funeral and natural grief at the loss of her grandsire, its substance dictated by memories of their frequent debates.

Looked at logically, the vision could be explained away

quite easily. Yet, she remembered all too vividly the sting of the flames, the throb of the other being's heart, the ache of his pain, the violence of his frustrated rage, to dismiss it as merely a vision caused by an empty stomach.

She attempted to lose herself in work, but found her songsculptures took on a life of their own. Whatever medium she chose, be it wood or stone, the natural lifesong she felt deep within the material changed upon completion into great flames, licking and caressing, desiring to consume all in its path.

She blamed the lifesong already present within the pieces, but knew the fault to be hers. That it was her own lifesong molding them, causing them to take on the shape of her nightmare.

Finally, she laid her work aside, accepting that this period of mourning, of adjusting, was obviously more protracted and powerful than she had previously imagined. And, until it had ebbed, nothing was to be gained from attempting normality.

She escaped down the narrow cliff path to the beach, her forever refuge, where strong winds sang loudly, and crashing surf beat frenzied time. Slipping off her clothes, she plunged naked into the starkly freezing waves.

The sea fought like a wild animal to claim her, buffeting her with icy cold fists of water. She threw her head back, exulting in the music of its cruelly magnificent strength. Fighting against its grip with all her might, thrilling as her body hummed with the sheer exhilaration of the battle.

At last she staggered to shore, spent yet refreshed; and hastily rubbed life into a body numbed from cold, pulling on clothes before falling to the sand in total abandonment, lifesong pulsing in every cell.

Her grandsire had feared every time she went to the sea, and she had understood his concerns. She was too young to remember the day her parents went out on its waves and did not return, yet knew the memory of that time was etched within his heart forever. Strong arms and soft voices, vague memories of laughter and loving embraces, were all the remembrances she carried of her parents.

Yet, her grandsire had raised her true, awakening skills which lay dormant within her, until the day she sang her first songsculpture into existence. Proudly, she'd run to show him the image she had created, feeling the connection to her lifesong, understanding her choice had been made. She was to be a songsculptor, as her parents had been before her and her grandsire before them.

The sand was hot beneath her spine, and she arched her body skywards, offering herself up to the sun, her mind blank and unfocused ... and it took her as speedily as it had before...

Eyes opened in another's head, looking, seeing, not understanding. A place, a room, unlike any she had ever seen before. Hard, rectangular lines of furniture, lit by a source she could not comprehend, it illuminated with no visible means of energy. No candle or oil lamp ever burnt with such a hard, steady light in her world. Her eyes winced away from its harshness.

Once again, she was a traveller within a host, was it the same one? Her instincts told her it was, and she became aware the being sat, slumped, in a kind of chair, its shiny, unforgiving black surface moved as he leant forward and rested his head in his hands. She felt pressure of skin on his forehead as he rubbed, felt the answering throb of pain in his skull, understood the ache, but was separate from it, a mere passenger within his mind.

He sat in fearful solitude. In the silence of aloneness, felt himself slipping back to that point, to then, to when he had lost everything to the flames. They licked at his being, keeping him prisoner in that moment, not allowing the agony to ever cease. He cried out, flailing with an uncoordinated hand, sending a glass crashing to the floor. His pain and anguish so raw, so immediate...she cowered away from its sharp edges, crawling to the furthest corners of his mind, curling up as small as she could make herself...

And opened her eyes once more to the brilliance of the sun, her thoughts a confusion of emotions, struggling to understand what had occurred, her lifesong pulsing in sympathy to the pain of another.

Sleep was elusive that night. In vain she closed her eyes in the darkness, willing the gentle oblivion of slumber to claim her, only for thoughts and images to crowd behind her lids, demanding attention.

Finally, she ceased trying and rolled onto her back. Tentatively, fearfully, she cleared her mind of all thought, reached out and waited...

Prepared for it this time, the transition was smoother, less shocking. Once again, she felt herself to be within the confines of the being's mind, saw the darkness of thought where the flames still lived. He murmured something incomprehensible, and she understood him to be gripped in the sleep of sheer exhaustion, the bedclothes beneath him crumpled and soaked, as his body twitched and fretted at torturous memories.

With rising panic, she sought for his lifesong, attempting to comfort and soothe him, to sing with him notes of calm and sympathy. Desperately, she reached deeper for his lifesong.

To find blankness, a void, nothing...he had no lifesong...

The absolute shock of it made her cry out in horror, shrinking away from such an aberration, fearfully groping for her own lifesong. Relief drenching her as she caught hold of its familiar rhythm, using its time and pace to quieten his racing heart, to calm the blood rushing through his veins.

He awoke with a speed which startled, his body catapulting upright, a hoarse yell echoing off sterile white walls. Suddenly, she was aware of his conscious mind, probing, questioning. He seemed aware of her, could feel her mind crouched within his, the song still quivering through his brain.

He arose from the bed and paced, cat like, across the floor, taking her with him into a smaller room, which, from its furnishings, she guessed to be where he performed his ablutions, but never had she imagined such things.

He pulled at a cord hanging from the ceiling. Instantly, bright draining light flooded the room, hurting her eyes. She blinked, felt his lids close, realised she could influence his movements, to a degree. He ran water into a basin from some sleek, shining device, splashed it onto his face, and she felt its chill, its wetness, and then the softness of the towel he used to dry himself.

He raised his head and stared into the over-sized mirror on the wall, and she stared back at himself, seeing him for the first time. Not so different from the men of her world, she thought, though paler of skin. He leant closer to the mirror, examining his face and she felt the shock of eyes of vivid blue, contrasting them in her mind with the topaz coloured eyes of her own people.

He moaned, and touched the cool glass with his hot forehead. Again, she felt pity well at his pain, singing softly to him words of love and hope.

Who are you?

His snapped words threw her backward. Somehow, it was as if she was free of his mind, that now she stood behind him, looking over his shoulder at his reflection in the mirror. Their eyes seemed to meet in the glass, and she saw the frown which tugged at his brow.

This is crazy, I'm going crazy, I thought, could have sworn...

He shook his head, his confusion plain, and she reached out and touched him.

Lilith?

The name was thrown despairingly at her, yet she knew, from the direction less focus of his gaze, that he could not see her as she saw him. He collapsed to the floor in bitter anguish...

And she awoke in her solitary bed, tasting the salt of her own tears...

Chapter Three. . .

Her thoughts returned to him constantly during the days which followed. She kept her mind occupied, did not seek to attain that state of thoughtlessness which seemed to herald the transition to his mind. Deliberately so, it had confused and frightened her, the experience of being so entrenched within another's mind, witness to his all-consuming rage and grief.

She wondered about him all the time, who he was, what tragedy had befallen him to render him so bereft and alone. Instinctively, she felt it to be connected to the fire she had witnessed, remembering his desperate struggle to free himself from those who held him back.

She thought about the name he had cried out, with such tormented hope it had torn at her heart. Lilith. Who was Lilith? Perhaps his mate, perhaps it was her loss he mourned. She tried to imagine losing a loved one, and not having the comfort of knowing they were now part of the great song, of feeling their presence still moving over and through your own lifesong.

She shuddered, tasting the rank tang of bile in her throat at the thought. How would one survive such a complete and utter loss without going mad?

Finally, alone in her bed one night, she did what she'd known all along she would do, cleared her mind, and returned to him...

He was alone again, sitting at a table. It took her a moment to realise this time she had not returned to her customary position within his thoughts. Instead, she was apart from his body, standing behind him, watching, trying to understand his movements as his fingers flew swiftly over some kind of device. Flat and sleek, made of a shining substance she could not distinguish, not wood or stone, it was like nothing she had ever encountered before, and she craned her neck curiously over his shoulder.

The length of her forearm, the device seemed to be made of two halves, with one half lying flat on the table. His fingers tapped industriously at the small buttons which were positioned on this half, and she saw they all carried strange, meaningless markings.

The other half of the device was folded up at an angle, brightly glowing with a strange white light, matching symbols to those on the lower portion appearing on it as his fingers moved. She watched, saw how his eyes never left it, as though it was imparting knowledge of great importance.

Tentatively, she felt for its lifesong, yet there was nothing. Whatever this device, it was not natural.

Curiously, she looked around, realising they were outside, on some sort of balcony. To her right was a massive window, and through it she could make out the room she had visited previously.

She turned to her left, and felt her heart almost stop

with wonderment. They were high, so high above the ground it made the cliffs overlooking her shore paltry by comparison, and, spread out before her, were ranks and tiers of what she assumed to be other dwellings, stacked on top of one another, jammed close, no space between them.

Her eyes grew wide at the sight. They were so numerous, never had she seen so many dwellings clustered together in one site. On her world, although some families did construct their dwellings close to one another, mostly people liked to maintain a distance around their homes, space to breathe, to be apart, room to feel the harmonies and rhythms of life flow through you.

But this...this vast forest of shining material and endless expanse of ever higher rooftops, this was like nothing she had encountered before, or ever imagined.

She turned away, discomforted, returning her attention to the man, reaching out for him with her mind, softly placing restful notes into his thoughts, curious to learn if flames still trapped him.

His fingers stilled and then stopped, as if he was aware of her presence. Emboldened, she pressed deeper, unable to explain to herself this fascination he held for her.

I feel you.

His words, murmured so low she barely heard them, shocked her. For a moment, she paused, her thoughts still entangled with his, then moved deeper within his mind, soothing and calming, showing him her intent was peaceful, her motives those of friendliness.

Who...what are you? You feel so real, yet I know you can't be. I know this must be some kind of dream, an hallucination, but, you feel so real.

I am real.

Finally, she spoke, unable to remain silent any longer, and he started in his chair, fingers flying to his temples, his eyes flicking wildly over his shoulder to look through where she stood.

How...where are you?

Behind you, within you, you cannot see me, but I can see you, I can feel you.

Are you a ghost?

She paused, considering his question. The concept of ghosts was not strange to her, indeed, the lifesong of the departed which echoed softly around that of the living, could perhaps be termed ghostly, but she did not believe this to be his meaning of the word.

I am not dead, if that is what you mean. I live, I am, I exist.

But where?

Far away from here, in another place, another world.

How is this possible?

I do not know. I only know my lifesong has brought me to this place, to you.

Lifesong? I don't understand, what's a lifesong?

The song which flows through each and every living

being, it binds and connects us all to life, to the universe and to the great song itself, to which we all, when we die, return.

Great song? What do you mean by that?

Can you not feel it? she cried out in a sudden passion, needing to make him hear, understand. *It is all around us, flows through and over us. Are you so deaf you cannot hear it? How can your species survive without it? Without a lifesong, surely you must all go insane. It gives life meaning, a purpose. If there is no music within you, then what is the reason for existence?*

He was silent, head bowed as if considering her words. Finally, when he spoke, his voice was low, empty with the bleakness of remembrance.

Perhaps you're right. Perhaps there is no meaning to life, at least, there's none left to mine.

The fire?

She felt his surprise, the sting of shock echoing through her own memories.

You know about that?

I was there, I saw, yet I did not understand.

My wife, my children...

He stopped, groaned with pain, then buried his head in his hands. She slipped from his mind, not wishing to invade his privacy, to bear witness to his pain, understanding the power of his loss. Perhaps a loss so strong it had found an answering resonance in her own grief and dragged her here, to this place, to him.

I am sorry...

She winced at the inadequacy of her words. Helplessly, she cut the connection and fled back to her own world, to that which was familiar and comforting...

Fervently, she vowed she would not return, all the while knowing she was lying to herself. She could not stay away, the hold he had upon her too strong to be ignored.

He filled her thoughts and movements. She began to work again, yet in every piece she sang into creation, she saw his face, the shape of his hands, the line of his jaw, the shockingly alien blue of his eyes.

People came, as usual, to barter their products for her highly sought after pieces. They looked at her creations, their expressions showing their confusion at such a radical change of style. Still, they must have had the power to please and intrigue, for, at the end of the day, every new piece had been exchanged and her cupboards were full of all the supplies she needed.

Then she mourned. All which had been inspired by him, all she had created, was gone. She worked long into the night, singing until her voice grew weak and hoarse. Then she slept. A dreamless, exhausted slumber, it left her body unsatisfied, fatigued and her mind foggy with distraction...

I knew you'd come back, at least, I hoped you would.

He rolled over on his bed, to look at where she lay beside him in the gloom of the dimly lit room. With a thrill of realisation, she knew he saw her.

You see me now?

Yes, that is...

He stopped, frowned, and she watched the play of emotions travel across his face. Although different from the men on her world, his face was still very pleasing to look upon, at least, she found it to be so.

I see something, a flicker of light, a shadow. Is that you, lying there beside me?

Yes.

She reached out, touched his cheek, saw his eyes widen, his own hand fly to his face in wonder.

Did you feel that?

I'm not sure. It felt like a whisper of breeze on a summer's day...

He stopped abruptly, plainly embarrassed, and she smiled, pleased with the imagery, glad of such proof of soul, for she had wondered. In the absence of a lifesong, could this man be considered to even be alive, to have a soul? It seemed so alien, so wrong, to reach out with her lifesong and feel nothing, no spark of resonance, no answering harmony.

What you said before, about there being no music in my world. You're wrong, we have music, lots of it, it's all around us, here, listen.

He arose from the bed, and she felt bereft at his absence, watching curiously as he touched the front of another strange device, this one gleaming black, and sound, music, suddenly issued from it.

She listened, pleased when he returned to the bed and once more lay beside her, his face turned towards hers, watching intently the space he knew she occupied.

Hear that? Music, my world is full of music, everywhere you go, there'll be music playing.

She sighed indulgently, seeking for the words to explain, without sounding as if she patronised or undermined in any way, not wishing to offend or cause him pain.

Yes, this is music, yet, it is not lifesong, it is not the great song. This is superficial, surface music, my world too is full of this music, created for enjoyment, entertainment...but, there is so much more, you cannot understand if you have never experienced it. A person's lifesong defines them, it gives shape to their talents, my lifesong has given me the power to create, to sculpt, and the pieces reveal their true shapes when I sing it forth from them.

She stopped, seeing from his baffled frown he did not understand. Inhaling lightly, she reached for his mind, flooding it with lifesong, sharing its joyous harmony. She showed him the music which filled her life, was always present, sometimes as nothing more than a background hum, sometimes a light, haunting refrain which lingered through thoughts and brushed lightly over emotions. She shared glimpses of the great song, reaching out with her lifesong, taking him with her, rolling in rhythm.

Together, they touched the stars, feeling the pulse of life at their fiercely burning hearts. With a thrill of discovery, she realised she was travelling further, faster, deeper, than ever before. Whole universes, millions of them, flashed by, insubstantial, fleeting, and, through it all, pulsed the great song.

Breathlessly, they landed back on the bed. Somehow, on their voyage, their hands had become entwined. She felt the rasp of his palm, skin against skin. Heard the hoarse sound of his breathing, unsteady and ragged, as it echoed in the stillness of the room.

She turned to look at him, saw the stunned wonder in his eyes, the flush of exhilaration on his cheeks. Slowly, as she watched, his breathing calmed, regained its even, steady pace. His eyes became focused, their vivid blueness losing the glaze of fantasy to fix on her, on her face, her body.

I see you, he murmured, his gaze roaming over each of her features, as though committing them to memory. *I see you quite clearly now, you're so beautiful. Your eyes, I've never seen eyes that colour before. I feel they could see right through me.*

Your eyes too are strange to me, yet. . . they are not displeasing.

They shared a smile, uncertain of what to say or feel. Then she felt a great wave of weariness sweep over her, as if their journey amongst the cosmos had depleted her lifesong. Her eyes closed.

No, wait...don't go! Dimly, she heard him cry out, then...

She awoke in her own bed to find Lani pawing at her, piteously demanding breakfast. It was dawn. All around she felt the lifesong of the creatures in the forest stirring, preparing to greet the sun and the start of another day.

Chapter Four. . .

Tell me about your world.

She did not answer him immediately, staring at the joining of their hands, marvelling at the feel of his skin, warm and familiar against her own.

Many times now she had returned to him, and, with each visitation, the desire to be with him had grown, until it was like a sickness within her blood, a yearning need to lay by his side. She ached to look into his eyes, to converse with him, their voices low and intimate, their gazes mingling as lovers do. Although they were not lovers, not yet.

My world, she mused quietly. *My world is very different. Not so busy, so frantic. You people seem to be never still, your minds are never at rest; constantly you strive and struggle for more.*

But surely, he replied. *That's how a race evolves and grows? It's that instinctive desire to survive, to improve our lives, that lifts us from mere animal status, elevates us into higher beings. If man had not always been driven by his needs and wants, we'd probably still be swinging from the trees.*

She was silent, reflecting on his words. Over time, she had become accustomed to the absence of lifesong, yet it never failed to disturb. That a whole race of people could apparently function and survive without any sense of the great song, without being connected, still amazed and appalled her.

The next day, she had a visitor. There was no warning, no message sent in advance, instead, he merely arrived in her workshop. There was just a sudden sense of his presence, a feeling in the skin on the back of her neck she was being observed.

She looked up, startled, attention drawn so abruptly from the piece she was singing into creation, its lines blurred, wavered. The sharp clear image she'd been striving for melting, the way ice does when touched by the first rays of spring sun.

He stood in the doorway of her workshop, his ancient form hunched over the simple carved staff he had used since before her memories began. She leapt to her feet, her stool twisting and falling, unnoticed, behind her.

'Honoured One,' she cried, and bowed, clasping hands to her heart in traditional homage to the most revered ancient of the elders. A lifelong friend of her grandsire, she had never been alone with him before. Now, awash with the greatness of his lifesong, the spacious workshop seemed close and confined.

'I am honoured by your presence,' she murmured, when at last she dared raise her eyes to meet his, still sharp despite the greatness of his years. They twinkled benevolently at her obvious discomfort, and the crevasses of life etched deeply into his face, creased still further into a gentle smile of welcome.

'Yes, yes,' he waved away her stiff formality, those sharp eyes darting around the workshop, at the finished pieces arranged on the shelves, at those which were still in transit, his attention catching and narrowing at that which had been inspired by the other place, by him.

Her breath held in her chest. She knew it could not mean anything to him, yet that gaze seemed all knowing, all seeing, as if he already knew much of what she was discovering.

'Very interesting,' was all he said. 'May I ask, what has evoked such a radical change in style? These pieces,' a wizened hand swept out, encompassing all, singling none. 'I have never seen their like before.'

'I...I felt it was time...for a change,' she murmured, nonplussed by his question. 'My grandsire's death, it seems to have triggered a change in direction...' her voice trailed away under the directness of his look.

'I see,' he nodded once, as if something of great importance had passed between them.

'Will you do me the honour of accepting some refreshment, wise one?' she asked, her initial shock fading enough for simple courtesy to be remembered.

She brewed tea, using petals from her precious hoard of the rare and highly valued gentianna flower. This beautiful, elusive plant grew only in the highest reaches of the mountains; and she remembered the old woman who had bartered them for one of her largest and most impressive pieces.

Thankful she had saved them, she breathed deeply of its calming, exotic aroma, pouring it carefully into her most delicate cups, arranging them pleasingly on a small, hand-painted tray, placing spiced biscuits on a matching plate.

The smallness of the gestures helped centre her. Smoothing her countenance into one of placid enquiry, she placed the tray on the small table before him, curling herself respectfully onto a stool close by. Watching silently as he took up a cup and sniffed, eyebrows raising in surprised delight.

'Gentianna tea? This is a rare and unexpected treat, I thank you.'

'You honour my dwelling, wise one,' she replied, then hesitated, wondering if she dared ask.

'What is your question, child?' he asked mildly, reaching for a spiced biscuit, crumbs scattering into the whiteness of his beard, eyes crinkling with obvious pleasure at the taste.

'I merely wonder at your presence,' she replied. 'I know your duties are many, and I am surprised, although, of course, deeply honoured, by your visit.'

'Your grandsire was my oldest and most valued of friends. Is it not natural I should pay a visit to his dearly beloved grandchild? To pay my respects, and to enquire into her...well-being?'

For a moment, her heart stilled at the knowledge she imagined she heard beneath his words. Then sense prevailed. He knew nothing, could never guess the secret which consumed her from within. Even the wisest could not imagine such a thing. A world without lifesong was unthinkable, inconceivable, a nightmare to be awoken from with fervent relief. No, the wise one's visit was a mere coincidence, a gesture of consideration for the grandchild of an old friend, that was all.

'I thank you for your concern, wise one,' she replied silkily, her expression as bland as his own. 'But I am well, my work keeps me much occupied...'

'Ah yes, your work,' he interrupted mildly, reaching for another biscuit. 'Is it not a little surprising, that the passing of a grandsire should provoke such an...extreme reaction? Such a fundamental change in style and context?'

'My grandsire and I were very close,' she countered, the tea hot and fragrant on her tongue. 'I believe it natural his passing should have awoken a desire for change in me.'

'Perhaps, perhaps,' the wise one mused. He paused, sipping thoughtfully at his tea. Silence, heavy and laden with expectation, settled upon them.

Uncomfortable under the directness of his gaze, she looked down at the smallness of her feet, studying in intricate detail the curve of her toes, the delicate carving of the rings she liked to adorn them with. And remembered, with a sudden flush of colour to her cheeks, the last time she had been with him, he had knelt at her feet, holding them wonderingly in his hands.

So small, he'd murmured. *So beautiful.*

She glanced up with a guilty start, to find the wise one's eyes upon her, felt the heat mount in her face. He could not know, only her reactions would betray her. Gently, she told herself fiercely, gently.

'Child,' his voice was low yet commanding. 'Is there something you need to tell me?'

'Wise one?' just the right note of puzzled concern in her voice.

'Your grandsire,' he continued. 'Was a good and intelligent man, wiser than you perhaps realise.'

'Yes, he was,' she murmured, confused by the conversational direction change.

'Were you aware, for instance, he was invited many times to join the council of elders?' Shock, painful and sharp, jolted through her. To have kept such a thing secret from her?

'I was not aware such an honour had been offered to him,' she replied carefully, masking her hurt behind a facade of polite curiosity. 'Tell me, wise one, why did he refuse?'

'He had his reasons,' came the obscure answer, and she frowned at a sudden thought.

'Was it because he had me to care for?' she asked

slowly, and the wise one shook his head.

'That may have been a factor,' he replied. 'But there were other, more pressing, demands on his time. Tell me, child, did your grandsire ever talk to you about things that possibly disturbed you?'

'Wise one?' This time she did not have to feign confusion.

'No matter,' he sighed, and finished his tea. Brushing crumbs from his beard he rose to go, pausing in the doorway to study her, his expression gravely serious. 'If you ever feel troubled by anything, or require my assistance in anyway...send for me, and I will come, day or night.'

'I thank you, wise one,' she said. 'But I do not see...'

'Anything,' he repeated, fixing her with a gaze of such intensity, she felt her soul revealed before it. 'Your grandsire was a very special man, as were your parents. You are their child, I feel an obligation to protect you.'

'Protect me, wise one? Protect me from what?'

'Remember,' he said, and was gone, leaving her uncomfortably wondering at the strangeness of the encounter, aware for the first time, of secrets from the past. Secrets involving her grandsire and, possibly, her parents?

She shook her head in confusion, longing for nightfall, when it would be safe to securely close the door to her dwelling and travel to that other place, to him, to a world which was rapidly becoming more real and more important than her own.

Chapter Five. . .

When night finally wrapped its velvet mantle around the world, she fled to him, impatient to touch, to feel. More unsettled by the visit of the wise one than she cared to admit, she felt an urgency grip her. When she opened her eyes and he was before her, she reached for him, hungry with need.

His eyes widened, yet he spoke not, merely let her take him where she would, slowing only when he realised it was her first time, holding back, gently soothing where she would have rushed. Quickly, her body learnt this new song, its rhythm pounding through her blood, singing through her heart and soul, their voices rising together in blissful harmony.

Later, they lay quietly, their bodies entwined.

Instinctively, she reached for him with her lifesong, yet found only emptiness, the smallness of his soul trapped within a single body. Disappointed, she sang to him, the wonder of the act of love empowering her song until it swelled and burst from its confines.

She heard him gasp, realised he could not accept such a joining, it was too much, it would burn him out from within. Yet, it would not be contained. For the first time, she ventured forth from his presence and the containment of his dwelling.

Onwards and upwards, she journeyed. Seeing his world, spread out in its entirety below her.

She danced and spiralled, flashing through clouds so fast she felt only the briefest touch of moisture on her cheek. She laughed aloud at such exhilaration, the sun warm on her face. The beauty of his world filled her with pleasure.

Reaching out with her lifesong she sought connections and found many. Hundreds, thousands, millions, billions. This world teemed with lifesong, as its creatures busied themselves with their lives.

She free fell, honing-in on the songs, picking out individual beings to share, for the briefest of moments, their existence and lifesong...

A great black and white seagoing mammal, leapt from the surface of a rolling mighty ocean, its lifesong exulting its joy to be alive. For a second she shared consciousness. In that second lived its whole life, felt the rush of salt water past its flanks, the thrill of twisting through the swell of the waves...

An ant, much like those on her own world, scurrying briskly to its nest. Its industriousness humbled her, the intensity of its need to care for its colony and its queen...

A coiled, basking snake, the sun warming its chilly blood, the scent of prey tasted in the air...

A small, rodent like creature, nimbly climbing behind the walls of a dwelling, whiskers twitching, fear pounding its heart, the desire for food driving it forwards...

A great, lumbering grey beast, baggy skin creasing

under a hot, unrelenting sun, the relief of wet mud, the tightly knit family community without which it could not survive...

A shining, leaping fish, desperately battling its way upstream, the urgent survivalist need to procreate forcing it ever upwards...

A bird, its wings glossy black, gliding on a thermal, surveying, hunting, the excited jerk of its body at the spotting of the smaller bird far below...

Another great sea mammal, this one large and ponderous, its lifesong an audible thing of beauty, booming out across the waves...

She lived them all. In that single moment, she lived all the lifesongs of the world, and it was glorious. For a second. Then, death and disaster crowded in.

Natural death was to be expected, it did not taint the great song, it was within the order of things, but this...this deliberate poisoning of the rivers and the seas...she gasped and choked with those that depended on the purity of its waters...

The annihilation of the mighty forests, the lungs of this world, the planet struggled to breathe, and she struggled with it, feeling the incomprehension and fear of the forest dwellers, fleeing before the obliteration of their homes, the great crying out of the trees which fell before their time...

The over-farming of the land, the stripping away of its

goodness and the choking of its natural defences with harsh polluting chemicals...

The fouling of the very air itself until creatures struggled for breath. In particular, a striped, winged insect battled to cope with the changes wrought in its world. As she shared, briefly, its lifesong, she realised the importance of this creature. That, should it be exterminated, the plants on this world would not be pollinated and would die, along with every other creature. All being so interlinked in an elegant and beautiful eco system of co-dependence, that removing one tiny, seemingly insignificant player from the scene, could result in extinction for all...

Everywhere she looked, was death and senseless destruction...a world being destroyed, raped, stripped of its assets. A world hell bent on ecological suicide...

Angrily, she searched for the culprit and did not have far to look. His race, his species. Hot urgent greed, the ambition she sensed within him. She saw it now, forced to bitter conclusion, saw the sweetness of the world trampled without heed or thought underfoot by a desperate need for more and more.

Screaming with horror, she recoiled from the image, retreating into herself, opening her eyes, to find herself staring into his concerned blue gaze.

Where did you go? he demanded, worry sharpening his tone. *Your body stayed here, but you...where did you go?*

Your world, she gasped, her heart still pounding with

the enormity of what she had seen. *Your world is so beautiful and yet ... you are killing it, taking and taking with no thought for tomorrow. Everything is dying, you are destroying it all, soon, there will be nothing left, nothing!*

Nothing left? he frowned. *No, surely it's not that bad? I know there are issues, the rainforests, some animals are close to extinction.*

You are all close to extinction! she interrupted with a cry. *Almost it is too late. Almost you have reached the point where it will be impossible to turn back, to save what is left! Oh, so much death and destruction! You are a planet of fools, you have but one world and you are busy destroying it. Don't you care? Can't you see what you are doing?*

Yes, but, he paused, plainly confused, agitated at the direction she had taken so soon after the sublime joining of their bodies. *But what can be done?* he demanded. *Tell me, what can be done to stop this? To save our planet?*

You must cease this brutal pillaging of your world's resources! Your planet is so rich, it could supply all you needed, were it managed and correctly harvested, respected. If you were to work with nature, instead of merely taking with no thought or heed for those who are to come after you.

But I am just one man! he insisted, his tone bitter with weary resignation. *What can I do, alone?*

159

It is true, you are just one voice, but surely there must be others? she pressed her hands to her heart, felt its frantic pulsing at the intensity of her need to convince him. *Perhaps, all it will take is for one man to say stop, enough, perhaps others will then have to courage to also speak out.*

Perhaps. He did not sound convinced, and she saw from his face she had failed to impress upon him the true scale of what she had seen, what she had felt.

He reached for her. Willingly she submitted, desperate to find oblivion in his body. To forget, if only for a while, the images still fresh in her mind.

Later, when the echoes of their cries of release had long faded from the room and he lay silently sleeping; she slipped quietly away to her own world.

Chapter Six. . .

She did not return to him for many days, needing the peace and tranquillity of her own world to restore and replenish her lifesong, which she felt had been depleted, tarnished, by its contact with the all-encompassing greed of his world.

She rested, sleeping deeply and dreamlessly every night, moving through the days slowly and deliberately. Not working, not seeing another living soul, enjoying protracted moments of stillness, when the vast rolling cadences of the great song lapped at her consciousness.

Finally, she felt strong enough to return to him, drawn by the needs and wants of her newly awakened body.

Craving him, his touch, his voice, his look. Yearning to feel again his body moving steadily and joyously within hers, she could not stay away another moment. In the unblinking of an eye, she was beside him, catching him on the cusp of asleep and awake.

He blinked in incomprehension, as she hungrily took from him that which she so ardently needed. Within moments, his urgency matched her own, and they plundered each other's bodies, riding the crest of splintering desire, their hands, mouths and hearts, locked in a dance as old as time, until they fell apart, sated and drained, their breathing harsh and ragged in the still, predawn hush of his room.

Once again, her lifesong soared free of the confines of

her body. Curious about his world, its people, she deliberately sought them out, probing, examining. Wishing to learn, to understand, how a race of people with no concept of lifesong could exist, and how an entire planet could have seemingly agreed on such a mutually destructive path.

An elderly woman lay in a small room, ripe with her squalid presence. She felt the woman's fear, tasted shock a revered and wise elder should be reduced to such an existence.

At the very last gasp of life, she felt the woman's dread of dying alone, of passing into nothingness, a life wasted and empty, offspring who wounded with unthinking lack of care. Heart brimming with sympathy, she gathered her lifesong and sung into the woman, soothing and calming, easing her transition over the threshold.

Moments, hours, later, the woman gave a great, shuddering breath. She felt her slip peacefully away, a blissfully happy smile lighting up her lined and wrinkled face, a smile which would ease the guilt of her family, when her body was eventually discovered, days later.

Angrily, she soared away, comparing this woman's miserable end with the respect and care elderly on her world were afforded. Valued for their knowledge, for the richness and potency of their lifesong, she knew the people of her own world would be shocked at the very idea of an elder dying alone, without the embracing loving arms of their family and friends all around them, and she bitterly wondered.

What kind of a world was this? That could treat its elders so.

A girl, little more than a child. She covered her eyes with her hands, as if this would be enough to hide her from his vicious intentions. Still, he found her, his violence brutal, shocking. She cried in horror, but fists were merely the beginning. Disbelievingly, she suffered with the child as her young, tender body was invaded, flesh bruising under the onslaught, sobs and cries for mercy falling on deaf ears.

Powerless to prevent the atrocity she was watching, she moved through the child's mind, smothering it under a blanket of blessed unconsciousness, filling the darkness with images of her own world, placing a tiny piece of her lifesong into the child's soul, so the truth of beauty and love would remain with the child for the whole of her miserable, mercifully short, existence.

She knew when the child awoke the horror of her life would still be there, yet, at least she had provided the child with a bolt hole, a refuge to escape to in times of extreme need.

She moved on, unable to bear it any longer, into the mind of another child, a boy this time, his body gaunt and stunted through the effects of lifelong, severe malnutrition. Barefoot and ragged, his hunger burnt as a constant, ignored fact, and around him she felt others like him.

Realisation dawned, in the absence of actual family, this disenfranchised little band of tattered urchins, had come together in a mutual joining of support and need. One that offered a rough and ready kind of love and stability.

She felt their fear, struggled to comprehend that this group of mere children were somehow prey. She saw men, identical in attire, track and follow the children. Not understanding, she watched as they pointed shiny sticks at them. There was a dreadful noise, and the children scattered, yet two did not rise. She saw the emptiness in their young old eyes, the spreading puddle of red beneath them, and knew they would never run with the pack again.

And then she perceived the shiny sticks were terrible weapons of some kind, weapons to rip apart the childish flesh of the innocent. Horrified, she moved on.

What kind of a world was this? That could treat its children so.

She found a building, large and imposing, it bustled with unceasing activity. Curious, she swept through it, recoiling at the tide of sickness and misery which threatened to engulf her, realising this to be a healing centre of sorts.

She saw and recognised the efforts of the healers to cope with the huge diversity and range of illnesses. Diseases of the mind and of the body, a few of which she recognised and could have healed herself in an instant, were she on her own world with access to her stock of powerful herbs and healing roots.

Many of the diseases, however, were shocking and alien, terrible disharmonies within bodies deprived of the natural restorative properties of their lifesong. Bodies which had turned on themselves, poisoning and contaminating their own precious organs, consuming them from within.

Comprehension dawned, without lifesong this world had turned to increasingly artificial and intrusive methods with which to heal their sick, causing new, more virulent diseases to be created, which, in turn, meant ever more extreme treatments had to be used, and so on and so on, a downward spiral of cause and effect.

The healers themselves were, on-the-whole, good people, committed to helping the wounded and the sick, but there were simply too many to cope with. She saw weary resignation amongst them, the unspoken acknowledgement they were merely fire-fighting, delaying the inevitable.

She saw much that sickened and bewildered her, people alone, afraid and in pain, left to call for help, unanswered, unaided, by healers too sick at heart themselves to come to their assistance. Hurriedly, she left.

What kind of a world was this? That could treat its sick so?

A baby, innocent and new-born. She peered wonderingly at its blank mind, rich with potential and possibilities, yet still the stain which tainted the rest of the world lurked within its soul.

The complete absence of lifesong seemed even more shocking than in the adults. She remembered the few times she had been present at the birth of new life on her own world. When the great song had rolled and gloried all around, heralding the triumphant renewal of life.

How different here. From the moment of birth until the last gasp of death, the people of this world struggled in a futile and pointless battle against themselves. Always at war, always at want. Greed and petty spite ate away at their souls until nothing mattered. She saw from the earliest point of life, children encouraged to strive and want, to take and dominate.

What kind of a world was this? That could treat itself so?

Abruptly, bone weary and sick to the soul of all she had seen, all she had experienced, she wished herself home, startled when she struggled to return. Used by now, to a smooth, almost imperceptible transition between worlds, this sensation of wading through clinging, dragging matter alarmed her, almost as if the contamination of his world had infected her, was dragging her down to its level.

It was with feelings of the greatest relief, she finally opened her eyes to find her own tranquil and peaceful dwelling once more cradling her in its arms.

Chapter Seven. . .

For many days after, it seemed she had carried back some of the despair and hopelessness of his world. Weary and chilled to the bone, she stayed within the refuge of her dwelling, huddled by the fire, eating little, fortifying herself with healing tinctures, wrinkling her nose at their bitter taste.

Her lifesong seemed weak, insubstantial, as if his world had drained some of her precious essence. Alarmed, she did not allow herself to travel back to him, giving herself time to consider all she had experienced, all she had learnt, allowing herself time to heal.

Great was her relief when, as the days slipped by, she felt her energy returning, until her lifesong rolled and swelled within her as strongly as before.

He called to her. Every night, as she lay, wide eyed and restless, in her narrow lonely bed, she felt him calling. His need and desire a tangible rushing force, it compelled itself across the void which separated them, tugging and insisting. At last, hungry for him, she overcame her fear and returned.

They did not speak. Words were unnecessary. Hands and mouths sought and found each other, bodies connected and re-connected. Again and again, she cried out in shocked, awed wonder at the gift of pleasure he gave.

Her body arched off the bed, taut as a bow, before

collapsing into boneless gasping ecstasy, clutching him to her, his breathing hoarse and ragged on her neck. Heart beat fiercely against heart as she realised, in that moment, how much she loved him, and how difficult it would be to leave him again.

For days she stayed with him, unthinking and uncaring of the shell of body she had left behind in her own world.

Fuelled by a mutual hunger, they existed in a kind of limbo, separate from either of their worlds, a time apart, where the only reality was each other and the urgent desire they had to touch, to hold, to love, to simply be.

And, when he slept, her soul soared upwards and away, morbid fascination forcing her to explore his world once again.

She saw...families struggling to survive, parents descending to any level to obtain food for their starving children...

She saw...perpetual warfare, whole races of people singled out to be slaughtered and discriminated against, the legacy of fear, intolerance and hatred being passed down through the generations. She saw children, so young their bones had barely had time to form, forced to take up weapons and fight.

She saw...individuals trapped in pointless, joyless existence, condemned to a treadmill of nagging petty discontent, until at last it curdled their souls and they crept noiselessly to their graves, leaving behind an uncaring world which did not even notice their passing. Wasted lives; wasted opportunities.

She watched in helpless disbelieving horror as half the world starved, whilst the other half gorged in a self-destruction of gluttony, their abused bodies bloated and miserable, their flesh groaning in desolation and self-loathing.

And everywhere, overlaying every scrap of existence was violence and the fear of violence.

Night after night, she travelled the world, forcing herself to look, to witness the atrocities the people of his planet visited upon each other and upon themselves.

Night after night, as she moved amongst them, she tried to touch as many unhappy souls with her lifesong as she could. Aware she could barely scratch the surface of the suffering, still, she tried.

Soothing damaged minds, comforting injured hearts, she looked for the neediest; the most desperate to aid, but the task was too vast. For the first time in her life, she felt the chill grip of despair.

And every morning she returned to him, exhausted and sick to her very heart, the blank desolation in her eyes conveying to him a taste of the horrors she had witnessed.

Scared for her, he pleaded with her to remain safely by his side. But, every night he would wake and realise she was not there, that only the shell of her being remained, cold and lifeless. He would wait and watch, fretful and anxious, until colour would return to her waxen cheeks and her beautiful eyes would open and stare at him, shocked and unblinking. Her gaze accusing, condemning.

He noticed how her peaceful contentment dimmed a little more with each passing day, how her flesh grew pale and her eyes dull. Worried, he begged her to stop, but she could not, her nocturnal wanderings as addictive as any drug, her need to try to heal these people becoming more urgent.

It was before dawn. Silently, she slipped into her body and opened her eyes. The room, his room, was dim, and she blinked several times before scattered senses could comprehend what she was seeing.

His back was to her, fingers moving in ceaseless energy over what she had been told was called a laptop. Unable to understand how he filled his days, she only knew he mostly worked from home, as she did, yet there any similarities between them ended.

He did not seem to create anything, either practical or beautiful. Concerned, she had asked him how he lived. With nothing to offer in trade, how did he eat, clothe himself and his dwelling?

His brow had furrowed, before clearing in relieved understanding.

Your society exists on a bartering system?

Yes, does not yours?

No, oh no, well, perhaps, amongst primitive people.
Primitive?

I mean, less socially advanced, he'd paused, seeing from her expression he'd offended, hurriedly he'd continued. *No, we work in exchange for money, and then we use this money to buy what we need.*

At first, the concept was confusing, then, with time, she had come to understand this system explained so much that was wrong with his world. Why some seemed to have so much, and some seemed to have so little. She had tried, haltingly, to clarify her feelings to him.

On my world, everyone has a talent, a skill. From childhood, their lifesong guides them towards this particular calling, be it making something practical, like clothing, or a necessary skill such as healing. Perhaps, a person has a talent for creating things of beauty, things people admire and want to adorn themselves and their homes. I am a sculptor, my lifesong enables me to see beneath the surface of a piece of wood or stone and sing forth its true shape. People like what I have created, and offer in exchange their own produce or skills.

He had been silent for a moment, thinking on what she had said. *What about if someone has no talent for anything?* he'd finally asked.

Everyone has a skill, even if it is merely for tending the earth, on my world, that is as valued as the most talented of healers. Everyone is necessary to maintain society and has an important role to play. On your world, there seem so many with no place, so many angry, frustrated disconnected beings. They feel society does not need them, so, in turn, they absolve themselves from the rules that bind a strong society together, becoming like monsters, hurting so much inside they must lash out at others in turn.

That's true enough, he'd replied ruefully.

Now, she lay quietly on the bed, attempting to re-connect with her lifesong, feeling the rawness inside, where pieces of herself had been torn out in increasingly smaller portions to aid the poor, wretched souls she discovered on her nightly travels.

Unaware of her return, he worked on.

Wearied beyond belief, she did not speak, did not let him know she had returned. Instead, her eyes wandered the now familiar room, finally alighting on the flickering screen on the wall. She knew its name, knew it to be a device which showed a confusing array of facts and stories. He had even attempted to explain to her how it worked, yet her mind had been unable to grasp the concept. In the end, she'd simply had to accept it was yet another example of how different their two worlds were.

The sound was muted. Sleepily, she watched as some vast, gleaming white piece of machinery forged upwards into a blue sky, and then an image was shown of a world, silent and beautiful, its blue seas wreathed in drifts of white. Shocked, she pulled herself upwards on the bed.

He turned at the sound, his expression registering relief at her return.

What is that? she asked, pointing at the screen.

Puzzled, he followed the direction of the gesture.

It's the Earth, he replied, simply.

What is the earth?

What is the...? Well, it's my world, this planet.

Yet, how are you seeing it? Without your lifesong to take you to the stars, without that connection to the great song, how is it possible for you to view your world?

We don't need a lifesong or whatever, there was a hint of arrogance in his tone. *Man has been to the moon, there are satellites in space, the space shuttle goes into orbit fairly regularly, there was even a space station up there.*

Satellites...shuttle? Confused, her words floundered. Patiently, quietly, he explained it all to her until finally she understood, and shrank back onto the bed in horror. *You seek to travel the stars without knowing the first thing about them?*

We understand them, he retorted, stung by the incredulous tone of her voice.

No, she shook her head adamantly. *You know nothing about them, how can you? Without the great song you are merely children, attempting to walk alone in the darkness, unsuspecting of what lies out there, or the harm you may do to others. Perhaps unintentionally, it is true, nonetheless, your race will blunder into the delicate structure of the universe, carrying your contagion with you.*

That's a bit much, he protested hotly. *You talk as if we're some kind of evil beings, monsters.*

You are, she replied flatly. *Oh, I know most of you do not mean to be, most of your race do not intend harm, yet still, harm others you must, it is the way your species has survived, at the expense of others. It is programmed into you, even within your babies; the need to satisfy self is the most overwhelming urge they possess.*

Exhausted, she lay still and closed her eyes, feeling his wounded silence in the room, unable to speak any more, to tell him of the beauty and majesty that lay out there, its intricate subtlety which could so easily be damaged or even destroyed.

Finally, he sighed, a heavy exhalation of concern, and moved to sit beside her on the bed. She felt it dip under his weight, yet extreme lethargy seemed to grip her and still she did not move.

Are you alright?

She sensed the moment his annoyance changed to concern. Touched, she attempted to reach out to him with her lifesong, to caress, to reassure. It was not there. Her eyes flew open, meeting his mildly worried gaze with a panic-stricken stare of her own.

What is it? What's the matter?

His voice was taut with anxiety, and she gagged on the lump of terror forming in her throat.

It's gone!

What is? What's gone?

My lifesong, it's gone, I can no longer feel it!

It'll come back, he reassured. *You know how weak you are when you return.*

No, this is different! she insisted. *Always before my lifesong was weak, yes, but still, it was there. Now, it's gone, I can no longer feel it, I'm no longer connected to the great song!*

Stinging tears welled in her eyes. Desperately she sought, deeper and deeper, probing violently for that which had been lost.

Attempting to console her, he pulled her into his arms. She fought him, clawing at her face and hair in soul ripping despair.

I feel nothing! she screamed. *I am nothing! How can you people live like this? So alone! So very, very alone!*

Sobbing, she finally allowed him to hold her, clinging to his body, her despair engulfing them both.

Later, the violence of the emotional storm abated, she lay quietly beside him. Numb with the horror of her loss, his words, meant to reassure and soothe, washed over her as if they were nothing.

Sleep, he urged her. *Rest, perhaps that's what your body needs. Sleep now, when you wake up, it'll be back, your lifesong will be back as strong as ever.*

She did not believe him, yet wanted to, clutching desperately at the hope. Closing her eyes, she felt the black pull of exhausted slumber, and allowed herself to tip over the edge into it.

Days drifted, and so did she. Time had no meaning, she simply existed. She felt his concern, his fear. It could not touch her. Softly, she was aware of all that she was, all she had been, all she could have become, melting away, like a snow sculpture left too long in the sun, her body liquefying, her features blurring. Without lifesong, there was no meaning, no cohesion to hold her together and so she began to let go.

On the fourth day, his control snapped. Striding to the bed, he gathered her up in his arms and shook her, his expression contorted with angry distress.

You can't go on like this. You must go home, perhaps there you can heal yourself.

I don't want to leave you, she dragged her scattered wits together to answer.

And I don't want to lose you, he stressed. *But neither can I sit here and just watch while you fade away. I can't let you die, not when there may be some way to save you.*

Going home may not save me, she murmured, and he released her back onto the bed, running trembling hands through his hair.

Maybe not, he agreed. *But, if you stay here you will definitely die; at least if you go back, there's a chance, maybe your people could help you, this wise one you spoke of, perhaps.*

Perhaps, she echoed softly. An image of the wise one's face, concerned and knowing, crept across her eyes. The thought occurred again, how much had he known? Looking back, it seemed he had been warning her, as if he'd somehow realised what she was experiencing.

You must go back, he said again. She looked at him, saw the worry etched deeply into his features, realised what it would mean to him if she were to die too, another loss, just like before. She had thought love would be enough to keep her here, now she understood she had been wrong.

Alright, she whispered, feeling the sting of hot tears inside her eyes. *But, I will miss you.*

I'll miss you too, he replied, his gaze steady and warming on her pale face. *But, at least I'll know you're alive somewhere in the universe and, maybe, one day, you'll be able to come back.*

Maybe, she agreed, but as she spoke the words understood them to be a lie.

Go now, he urged. *Go before you become so weak you can't.*

I love you. She gave him the words as a parting gift, saw the smile slip onto his lips as she closed her eyes, and felt for the link.

I love you too. She heard him as she reached out with everything she had, seeking that strong silver thread which always pulled her home. Over and again she probed, searching, grasping, fumbling for it, but it was like trying to find a needle in a dark room. In despair, she opened her eyes once again to his face.

Go, he urged. *You must go.*

I cannot, she sobbed. *The connection is broken, I can never go home!*

Chapter Eight. . .

Cold, she was so cold. Huddled beneath piles of covers, her body now barely enough of a presence to raise them more than a few inches, she moved in and out of a fugue state. In her more lucid moments, she wondered what was happening to the outer husk of the body she had left behind on her own world. Was it too dying, withering away like an un-watered plant?

Vaguely, she was aware of him moving about the room. Often, he came to her side. Once she heard him sobbing and pacing, railing at some god. She wanted to comfort, to assure him it was not his fault, that she had chosen this path. The effort to move was too much. Gratefully, she let the darkness close over her once again.

Suddenly, she was jerked from her state of lethargy as he threw back the covers and lifted her, gently thrusting her arms into sleeves of a large, woollen garment, slipping thick socks onto her feet.

Feebly, she protested, her hands fluttering to his arms, like a bird's wings beating on a windowpane.

Come on, he said. *Please try to help me. We must go out and it's so cold, you'll need to be well wrapped up to keep you warm.*

No, she murmured. *Where? Leave me alone, let me die in peace.*

I couldn't just sit here doing nothing, he stated flatly. *So, I googled lifesong, I didn't expect to find anything, but*

I did, I did.

His words were strange, meaningless. Numbly, she stared at him.

There's a place, he continued. *A sort of retreat, almost what you'd call a monastery, only not religious, well, not a recognised religion. It didn't have its own website, from what I can gather they shun all modern technology, but the founder once gave an interview, that's what google took me to, the interview, and in it he says the aim of the retreat is to attempt to reconnect people to their lifesong.*

He cannot mean lifesong in the true sense, she whispered, her mind dazed by his words. *He cannot, it must be a coincidence.*

Probably, he agreed, wrapping a thick, well lined coat around her wraith-like form. *But it's worth a try, anything is better than just sitting here, watching you...*

He stopped and swallowed hard, busying himself with placing a warm scarf about her neck, a hat upon her head. In her mind, she completed his sentence...anything was better than sitting there watching her die. She realised in an instant she must allow him to do this, that his very nature would not tolerate inactivity. In all her nocturnal travelling around his world, she had come to understand his species a little, and knew passive acceptance was not a prevalent trait.

There's no email, no phone, he continued briskly, leading her towards the door. *But, there's an address and it's not too far away, about thirty miles. If we go now, we'll miss the traffic.*

Very well, she murmured, leaning against him heavily, her strength almost completely gone.

Outside the door to his home stretched a long, dimly lit corridor. Unable to deal with any more unfamiliar stimuli, she merely closed her senses to it all, turning her face into his shoulder, as he led her into a small, box like room, lined with mirrors. For the first time, she saw herself as she appeared to him - so thin, so insubstantial, her huge topaz eyes the only alive part of her features.

The floor lurched and she uttered a breathy cry, clutching at him for support, feeling their rapid descent with disbelief and terror. Softly, he reassured, holding her steady, lending his strength.

When the box room finally stopped, an eternity later, she was relieved when the door silently slid open to reveal a dark subterranean world filled with fantastical objects.

Numb with incomprehension, she watched in silence as he lifted his arm and pressed a small item clasped between his fingers, catching her breath when one of the strange objects abruptly flashed lights at them and uttered a strange clicking noise.

He took her to it, opening a part of it to reveal seats inside, comfortable, well padded, and she slid gratefully down into the object, feeling the give of leather beneath her. Gently, he fastened some sort of strap across her chest and lap, before closing the door. Hurrying round to the other side of the object, he clambered into another seat, identical to her own, yet placed behind some sort of wheel.

The small device with which he had awoken the object, he now fitted into a hole located under the wheel, turned it and the object burst into throaty angry life.

Unable to control herself, she moaned with fear, grabbing the edge of the seat, turning large terrified eyes upon him. *What is this thing?* she gasped, feeling her heart thud with anxiety as the object began to move.

It's called a car, he replied.

A car? But how...?

Look, he interrupted, his manner almost brisk, and she sensed his relief that finally he was doing something. *Do you have carts, wagons on your world?*

Carts? Yes, of course.

Well, think of this as a kind of mechanised cart.

Oh, I see.

And she did see, understanding his race would never be satisfied with the simple yet infinitely practical cart. They would always strive to make it quicker, faster, better, until eventually they arrived at machinery which could explore the stars.

Stars. As they left the underground cavern and emerged into the crystalline beauty of a wintry night, she tipped her head back and saw, through the curiously pointless window above her head, the dazzling canopy of stars spread out across the inky black sky.

Different from the constellations viewed from her world, without the connection to them her lifesong would have afforded, looking at them was like catching glimpses of freedom through the bars of a prison, tantalising, but unreachable.

It's about an hour's drive, he stated, handling the car skilfully, moving to avoid the other cars that, even at this late hour, thronged all around them.

Why don't you try and get some sleep?

Nodding, suddenly weary, she rested her head back against the comfort of the padded leather seat, feeling her eyelids droop and sleep claim her.

A thin grey dawn had broken when she awoke, neck stiff from too long in one position, mind clouded from deep, dreamless sleep. For moments she merely blinked, becoming aware the car had stopped moving and he was gone.

Panic had her pulling herself upright, searching for him, finding him standing before a large pair of imposing, solid looking wooden gates. His back to her, he appeared to be arguing with a solemn faced young man who peered at him through a small window set in the impenetrable mass of wood.

Wishing to be with him, her hands beat uselessly at the door. Unable to discover how it opened, by chance she pressed a button, the glass window pane slid down and their words floated to her on the still air of the early morning.

You have to help us, please...she's dying!

Well, take her to a hospital. This is a closed order, no visitors.

Please, we've come so far.

I'm sorry, there's nothing we can do to help.

She heard the steel in the young man's voice and knew it to be over. Their last hope, if indeed it had ever been a hope, had come to nothing.

In despair, she leant back and closed her eyes, reaching out with every fibre of her being in one last attempt at a connection to anyone, anything. She did not want to die all alone, so far away from home.

A spark of life flickered within her, small and inconsequential, still, it was the best she could manage and she flung it from her, out into the world, hoping against hope some creature would take pity on her, would offer a scrap of comfort in her last, desperate moments of life.

A chord, a resonance, for a second only it seemed to her she felt an answering echo. Faint, so faint though, as if, far away, something had heard and understood, had maybe even sent a soft reply. It was too little, too late, with a sigh her head fell forward.

Dimly, she felt the car door being wrenched open, his arms around her, undoing the strap which bound her, holding her close to his chest, his sobs echoing in her ear, his breath warm on her neck.

Please, he moaned. *Don't go, don't leave me!*

Wait.

Her eyes fluttered half open, it was the young man from the gate. Wearing an expression of intense puzzled disapproval, he strode towards the car. She frowned slightly, his clothes, what was it about his clothes? For some reason, they reminded her of home.

You must come with me, the young man ordered. *He wants to see you.*

Too weak to stand now, she was carried hastily inside the enclosure. Dimly aware of silent echoing corridors, of a room, still and peaceful, of a figure waiting, waiting for her. He turned at their approach, his hand reaching for her, his touch on her brow soothing. Then she felt it. A whisper of lifesong. It trickled into her, a tiny stream of essential, life renewing energy and she gulped at it, like a person dying of thirst at the first taste of water.

*But, that's impossible...*she murmured, and the stranger smiled.

Oh child, you poor lost child...

The room in which she awoke was very pleasing. Simply furnished, it reminded her of home and this comforted her. She stirred in the narrow bed and he turned away from the window at the sound, relief leaping into his eyes. She wondered how long he had stood there, how long she had slept.

Where am I? What happened? she asked, probing her mind for memories.

You've slept for so long, he replied, his face crinkling with love as he moved to sit beside her on the bed, helping her to sit. *We're in the retreat still, the teacher, he, well, I'm not sure what he did, he touched your head, it pulled you back, you were so close to death, I could see it on your face.*

The teacher? she murmured enquiringly.

Yes, that's what he's known as, apparently, he pulled a rueful face. *Frankly, he can call himself whatever he pleases, I'm just relieved he could help you.*

She nodded slowly, remembering the incredible, impossible feel of his lifesong, faint, barely there, yet it had been enough to stop her slipping away, enough to hold her here, for now.

He wants to see you, he continued. *When you're ready, he wants to see you again.*

The same steely eyed young man led them again to the room she had only the vaguest memories of. Its aura one of peace and warmth, she felt the sunlight as it streamed through the windows, stirring her chilly blood. Blinked at the dust motes which danced in the columns of light, as they slowly paced towards the still, expectant figure that awaited them.

A hands breadth away she stopped, he was a stranger to her. Yet, something called, something nagged at her to remember.

Do I...do I know you? she asked, her voice a whisper, and he smiled, his expression wistful almost sorrowful.

Once, perhaps, he murmured. His hand rested on her brow and she felt it again, that faint flicker of a lifesong, tantalising and elusive.

On her world, the possessor of such a weak lifesong would be considered close to death, or a creature of the lowest denomination, but here, on this barren and soulless planet, it was as welcome as an oasis would be in the midst of a heat scorched desert.

But there was something else, something in the very nature of the lifesong itself, something long forgotten, something familiar.

How is this possible? Here, on this world, where the creatures of the sea, sky and land all have lifesongs and yet none of its people do. I thought myself alone...

And yet, here I am, he mused, then, reaching his hands to his face, he passed them over his eyes, doing something she did not understand. His hands fell to his side, and she stared with disbelief into his topaz gaze.

Father?

Chapter Nine. . .

I do not understand. How is it you are here? They sat before a fire, its glowing heart casting living shadows of heat over their faces. Wonderingly, she turned to look at her father, her hand still clasped tightly in his, the expression in his eyes warming her every bit as much as the fire.

What did your grandsire tell you?

Nothing, that is, nothing that would explain your presence here. He told me you had died, at sea, along with my mother...

She let the name linger in the air between them, needing an answer, yet reluctant to ask outright. He sighed, the affection in his eyes for her, dimming into sorrow for the loss of his love.

Your mother died, shortly after we were stranded here. She was simply not strong enough to survive without her lifesong.

As I was not?

As you were not, he agreed. *Maybe it is inherent in females; that need for connection, the despair of loneliness. It is something which still requires a great deal of study, perhaps if I...*

Please, she begged, dragging his attention back. *Please tell me how you came to be here, how I came to be here. What happened to us?*

It has long been known our family is...different from

others, he began. *Our lifesong is powerful, and yet, it is not only that, it seems to enable us to travel further than any other, to seek out mysteries. That desire to explore, to know, to understand, it is an overwhelming trait of our bloodline.*

Yes, she murmured in agreement, reflecting on her life, the constant questioning of her grandsire, her need to understand all around her, their heated debates on life on other worlds. Never had she repeated these discussions to another living soul, only now did she question her motives for keeping it secret. Was it because she had known, instinctively, none besides themselves would have understood?

Your grandsire, my father, had dabbled with such explorations, projecting his mind further and further; attempting to make contact with lives on other worlds. His efforts though, all seemed doomed to failure, until we...for by that time I was working alongside him...we discovered it was possible to project not just your mind, but your essence as well. That the body could be split into four components, not three as had previously been believed, your soul, your mind and, of course, your physical outer shell, but there was a fourth, inner layer, like a membrane, a skin beneath the skin, which could also be projected, along with your soul and your mind, leaving just the outer husk, the shell of your physical body behind.

Like an onion, her lover, silent until now, murmured behind them, and her father turned pleased eyes upon him.

Yes, that is an entirely accurate analogy. We discovered our body was made of these layers which could be separated, like an onion, and our family, alone amongst our species, had this ability.

So, this fourth layer, this membrane, this is what I am now? She asked, touching her cold skin disbelievingly, seeing for herself how insubstantial, how translucent, it appeared.

Yes, it promotes just enough physical presence to allow you to feel and touch, and to be touched in return, he concluded, mouth twisting in a wry grin as he glanced over at her lover. She felt a momentary flush of discomfort, knowing he had accurately guessed at the relationship between them.

So, you travelled to this world?

Yes.

With my mother?

Yes.

But how was that possible? You said only those of our bloodline had the ability?

That's true, but your mother was the child of your grandsire's sister, so she shared the same bloodline. All the same, she did not possess the ability I did. She could travel, but only if I accompanied her, she lacked the strength to even attempt the task herself.

What happened to her? she asked slowly, needing to know, yet at the same time, afraid to hear.

Something went wrong, he met her gaze with steady, regretful eyes. *I miscalculated, we stayed too long, the malaise on this world infected us and dissolved the link. By the time I realised what was happening, it was too late. I tried to send your mother back alone, but it was no use. The thread which tied us to our physical bodies was gone, and we were too weak, our lifesongs too drained, to even attempt the journey unaided.*

For long moments he remained silent, his stare hooded and turned towards the flames, as if remembering things buried deep, things that pained to be recalled.

For weeks we remained in hiding, resting, praying our lifesongs would recover. They never did. Gradually, your mother grew weaker, until she simply faded away and was gone. For days, I clung to the hope that perhaps the dissolution of her presence on this world was enough to somehow catapult her back into her body on our own. But, had that happened, I knew my father would have found some way to reach me. Perhaps he could not have managed it alone, but, with the combined lifesongs of the council of elders, he would have been able to...

The council of elders? she interrupted him, startled. *Did they know what you were doing?*

Of course, he replied, surprised. *We would never have*

attempted such a thing without their permission and guidance. Indeed, were it not for their generosity in providing for us, so we did not have to be concerned with our everyday needs, it would have been more difficult for us to find the time.

Funding the space project, her lover murmured, and her father started slightly in his seat, then looked thoughtful, nodding his head, as if in sudden realisation.

How did you survive? she asked, reaching to take his other hand in her own, feeling the warmth of his touch in stark contrast to the coldness of her own.

I do not know, he replied slowly. *Perhaps, being male, I was naturally stronger than your mother. I only know that I did survive, and, gradually, I began to make a life for myself on this poor, benighted world. My lifesong did not return, and the tiny scrap I had remaining I hoarded jealously, understanding, should it ever completely deplete, I too would simply dissipate into nothing.*

But, you gave some to me, she cried, horrified at what this might mean.

The tiniest whisper, he dismissed her worries with an airy wave. *Do not fear, I have enough still.*

She nodded, still concerned, then looked around the room, aware of the strangeness of the place she had found him in, and remembering the young man who had admitted them.

Father, what is this place? What have you become?

I am the Teacher, he proclaimed, a little pompously, she thought. *I guide and teach others, help them to re-connect with their lifesong. I attempt to awaken long dormant memories and skills in these people, so that they may once again take their places within the great song.*

Is such a thing possible? she exclaimed in surprise, remembering her own experiences, the complete lack of any suggestion of a lifesong within these soulless entities.

I believe so. He leant forward, clutching her hands tightly in his intensity. *Think of it. Think of what it could mean. If these people could be returned to the light, perhaps the terrible sickness of self which has infested this planet for millennia could be lifted.*

Yes, she breathed, caught up in his vision. *They could be saved...*

We don't need saving! her lover's voice, flat and angry, intruded into their shared moment. Almost annoyed she turned upon him.

But you do! she replied passionately. *You need saving from yourselves. Your whole world, this planet, you are killing it, slowly and terribly, it has been raped and mutilated until it can bear no more.*

That's a bit harsh, he retorted, yet she saw by the way his eyes would not meet her own, that he heard and recognised the truth in what she said.

Is it? Her father's calm voice defused the heat rising between them. *Is it not time to recognise the truth,* he continued. *To admit to what you have become...*

And what have we become? Her lover demanded hotly.

A race of self-obsessed and greed driven beings. You consume without heed for consequence, you destroy that which you need to survive. A species that breeds without the need for conjoining...

Conjoining? her lover's voice was confused, hastily she explained.

It is the means by which children are conceived on my world. Children can only be born to couples who reach a level of complete loving harmony, the child must be wanted equally by both, or conception does not occur, it ensures every child is loved and nurtured.

How very different on this world, her father remarked, his tone silky with almost sarcasm. *Where children are bred indiscriminately, born to lives of poverty, violence and neglect. Yet, it was this ability to breed vast numbers of offspring which tipped the balance in your species favour, that, and a ruthless, single minded desire for self-advancement. Survival of the fittest, I believe you call it, but that is merely a term to hide what your species are...*

That's not true! It's just not true...We're not... I mean...

Her father raised his head, regarded her lover steadily, until he looked away in shameful acknowledgement. Her heart moved by his miserable silence, she placed her cold hand over his, touched by the fleeting look of gratitude he shot her.

Tell me about your students, she urged her father, desperate to defuse the ominous, angry atmosphere which lay over them. *Tell me of your work.*

It has taken many years, but I have gathered around me those who perhaps, out of all the people on this world, have an inkling of what they have lost, a racial memory if you will, of what they once were. Together, we have chosen to remove ourselves from the toxin of this world. We study, meditate, and attempt to reach within ourselves to tap into the core of lifesong which I believe still lies buried, locked away, within each and every person.

And are you successful? she asked, intrigued by the vision his words created.

Sometimes, there is a spark, a glow. Some of my more advanced students report feeling a pulse, a rhythm. We have hope, and I feel the very act of trying to attain their lifesong, may help the people of this planet to finally be at peace with themselves.

But you are merely one, she murmured. *How can you possibly hope to reach them all?*

This is but one of the sanctuaries I have created on this world, he told her, his voice touched with pride. *There are another seven led by my most promising students, I travel in turn to each. It is fortunate I happened to be in this place when you crossed over, or, it is possible my presence acted as a beacon, calling you to me.*

Father, once again she clasped his hands in sudden enthusiasm. *Now that I am here, I want to help you, help these people. I too have seen the suffering and unrest that plagues them. I would like to assist you in your work, perhaps together...*

No.

Her father's flat refusal shocked and dismayed her. Hurt, she pulled her hands away from him and leant back in her chair.

My daughter, I would wish nothing more than to spend my life with you and share my work, but, you cannot stay here. Already, the scrap of lifesong I placed within you is diminishing, I am aware of this, even if you are not. Soon, it will be gone, and then you will die. No, you must return.

It's impossible to return, she cried. *I tried, so hard, but the link was gone.*

The link is still there, he reassured. *You were just unable to feel it, the sickness infecting this planet has numbed your ability. But, hopefully, with my help, and with the combined efforts of my students, we may be able to send you home.*

Chapter Ten. . .

All was ready. She felt comforted by her father's confidence, but then, hidden behind his eyes, she saw concern and was afraid.

She feared they would fail in the attempt and her thin scrap of existence would be extinguished, snuffed out like the flame of a candle. She feared in this desperate attempt to return her home, her father's remaining dregs of lifesong would be drained, and she feared his students, all those earnest, gentle souls who watched her with eyes of wonder and awe would also somehow be harmed.

Her lover stayed close, his rock like presence a source of strength and determination. Each time her eyes strayed to his, the truth moved between them. Succeed or fail, after this night they would no more be together.

When her father had declared his intention, and hurried away to alert his students to make their preparations, she had taken her lover by the hand and led him to the room she had awoken in. Bolting the door, she had held him to her one last time, and their souls and essences had mingled in one final sublime joining, attaining a level of harmony never-before achieved, their cries of passionate relief merging into sorrow at the parting that was to come.

Now he stood beside her, a warm hand closed firmly over her iced fist, and his silent contemplation of the activity in the room somehow soothed and centred her.

A fire burnt on a large central hearth around which the students sat in a circle. Deep in meditation, their eyes were open, but no longer saw. Voices murmured together in a chant she recognised, it was the chapla, the calling to self of the great song. The low, wordless tones set her heart beating with a fierce response and she felt her pulse, shallow and uncertain now, peak with anticipation.

Softly, her father beckoned to her. It was time.

She turned to her lover.

You have to go, he murmured and she nodded, unable to speak past the lump that threatened to choke her. *I promise,* he began, emotion husking his voice. *I promise to try and make a difference, I will help your father. Perhaps, the two of us can make a difference.*

She nodded and he fell silent, holding onto her hand as if he would never let go. Behind them, her father cleared his throat, reluctantly they released hands and stepped apart.

Without words, they gazed at each other, filling their hearts and minds one last time. He touched her face gently, before turning her towards the circle, towards her father. Stepping back from her, she knew he was of her past now. Resolutely, she squared her shoulders and moved to her father's side.

Holding out a hand, he dropped a bundle of herbs onto the fire and instantly fumes, choking and all consuming, snatched at her lungs, greedily sucking at her breath.

She gasped, afraid, then felt her father's grip on her shoulders. Firmly he held her over the smoke and she inhaled deeply, the chanting of the students seeming to increase in pace and intensity.

She blinked...and was elsewhere...moving through time and space. She searched for the silver thread, but could not see it. Panic gripped, and she fought against the force which dragged her relentlessly on, terrified, wishing only to return to her father, to her lover.

Softly, child, softly...the voice was everywhere and nowhere, it moved through and around her, it was ancient and of now, it was all powerful yet benevolent, and she relaxed, instinctively knowing it meant her no harm.

Who are you? she cried, or perhaps merely thought. *Where are you? What are you?*

Do you not recognise me? It demanded, and she felt the notes thrum through her blood and her bones, felt the pulse of life beat steady and true within her body, heard the rhythm pulse through the very fabric of existence.

The great song...she breathed, and felt its glow of almost humour.

That is one of my names, it mused.

Tell me, show me! she demanded.

Ah child, what would you know?

Everything! she cried recklessly, giddy with its presence.

So, it took her, and showed her...whole universes

moving ceaselessly within the inky blackness of space, planets throbbing to the beat of lifesong all worshipping the great song. She saw it in its many guises, all benign. Saw whole worlds bathed in its light and she laughed aloud at its magnificence.

But there were other worlds from which no light came. Plunged into perpetual gloom, they were scattered and few, but she saw how potent their infection was. Moving on, she saw her lover's world, a world she had come to care greatly for, crouching in its own foul cloud of darkness.

What causes this? she cried, and it showed her. The Other. Insidious. Dark. Malicious. A direct counterbalance to the great song, it crept amongst the stars searching for prey. Nameless, formless, it was mostly unsuccessful, but a few, a precious few, listened to its oily promises and made deals which condemned their species forever.

The great song whirled the dust of millennia, and she saw her lover's world as it had been. Teeming with lifesong, all species existing in perfect harmony; all equal in the eyes of one another. She saw the darkness reach the young world, its subtle searching of their souls, the filthy bargain that was struck.

Paradise was lost. Their lifesongs suppressed forever, the darkness fed off its power, and, in exchange, their race became consumed with the urge to survive and triumph at any cost. She saw the need for conjoining overcome; the hoards of children bred to swarm like a virus over the surface of the planet.

She saw other species exploited for want and need. She even saw the other humanoid races which shared their world hunted into extinction. One race hung on for longer than the others, heavy of brow yet pure of lifesong, they fled further and further from the new violence of her lover's race, but it was no use. The planet was no longer big enough to contain the two species.

Crying out in grief and horror, she looked away and the great song whirled her through time. She was comforted by the sight of millions of worlds flooded with its pure, blinding light. But, the darkness was always there, waiting, ready to spread its message of greed and hate.

You must be strong, child, the great song murmured through her bones. *Much depends on you.*

The subtle yet persistent pressure suddenly ceased. For a moment, she was floating over the chamber where students chanted and a fire burned. She saw a shadow of her body begin to solidify in her father's arms.

No!

She felt him cry out, saw the herbs he desperately threw onto the fire, the increased vigour of the chanting hurled her back once more, jerking upwards and away from her lover's world, then floating, uncertain and afraid.

The darkness was absolute, the only relief a thin, so thin, strand of silver thread stretching away into the distance.

She followed it, heart pounding in an all-consuming fear, until suddenly it faded, ended in nothing. She stopped, lost and alone in the silence, abandoned by all, unable even to hear the great song.

Help me!

She screamed aloud, twisting in the darkness, too afraid to go on, unable to go back, stranded between worlds, her strength failing, her lifesong withering, dying.

Wait, what was this?

An echo, a melody, subtle yet insistent, it pulsed through the darkness. Gratefully she felt for it, feeling it grow stronger in its intensity the more she moved towards it. Throbbing through her heart and brain, it spoke of home and security, of safety and love.

Joyfully, she slid along it and, in a burst of light, saw her room on her world.

Her body, pale and wraith like, lying upon the bed, and, surrounding it, a solid circle of the council of elders, their lifesongs reaching into the darkness, pulling her to them, dragging her home. Gasping in shock, she landed with a thud inside her body, and opened her eyes to the relieved steady gaze of the wise one.

'Welcome back,' he said.

For the first three days after her return, she slept the sleep of the dead, only awakening to consume vast quantities of food, her malnourished body desperate to reclaim all it had lost.

And, on the fourth day, they took her to see her father. Leading her deeper and deeper into the furthermost reaches of the caves sacred to the council of elders, she had felt the power of the lifesong oozing from its walls. Realised the sanctity and strength of the place.

Finally, they reached the deepest cavern and there, surrounded by a circle of chanting elders, lay her father. Wonderingly, she approached, knelt by his side, gently touched his translucent skin, stroked his barely-there hair.

'We did not know if we were helping him at all,' one murmured to her. 'Maintaining his body, feeding his soul with constant lifesong. We were too late to save your mother, but we hoped, that maybe, we were helping in some way...'

'You are,' she reassured them. 'Oh, believe me, you are. '

Much had been spoken of in the months since her return. The council of elders had listened and questioned, until every single morsel of information had been extracted from her experience.

Their countenances darkened at her story of the infection which had claimed the lifesongs of other worlds. As she told of all that the great song had shown her, had told her, they had exchanged glances of deepest despair.

Finally, she returned to her home, to her quiet, simple life, moving through her days much as before. Yet, all was different now.

Today, the wise one came to see her. After the usual niceties of greeting and the ritual of tea had been observed, he sat with her on the bench outside the dwelling, watching the sun set over the sea.

'It has been decided to tell the people nothing of this,' he declared.

She was silent, waiting for him to continue.

'After all, this other world is so far away, it will take millennia before they could possibly reach us with these ships of space you spoke of. By then, who knows, maybe a cure will have been found against the infection they carry.'

'Maybe,' she agreed quietly.

But, after he had gone, as she held her baby close to her breast and gazed down into the bright alien blueness of his eyes, she thought of her lover's world, of its people, of their drive and determination, of the unceasing, always present need that spurred his race to forever stride for more and more.

Somehow, she did not believe they would have that long...

The End...

Time No More

When dragons sing and angels cry
Then will the world be ended.
Time will stop, there is no more
It cannot now be mended.

An end to sorrow, no more pain
The dragon's song will soothe us.
The world is finished, no more light
Just dark eternal, endless.

Do not fear the dark my child
And weep and ask me why.
All mortal things must have their time
All mortal things must die.

When dragons cry and angels sing
Then is the world re-born.
But not for man, he's had his chance
Another age will dawn.

About the Author

Julia Blake lives in the beautiful historical town of Bury St. Edmunds, deep in the heart of the county of Suffolk in the UK, with her daughter, one crazy cat and a succession of even crazier lodgers.

She's been writing all her life, but only recently took herself seriously enough to consider being published. Her first novel, The Book of Eve, met with worldwide critical acclaim, her second novella, Lifesong, a fantasy/sci-fi story, is causing a stir with its powerful, environmental message, and her third novel, Becoming Lili, is set to become the must-read book of the summer.

Julia leads a busy life, juggling working and family commitments with her writing, and has a strong internet presence, loving the close-knit and supportive community of fellow authors she has found on social media, and promises there are plenty more books in the pipeline.

Julia says: 'I write the kind of books I like to read myself, warm and engaging novels, with strong, three dimensional characters you can really connect with.'

35893343R00120

Printed in Great Britain
by Amazon